"If Marvin says he'll ride down
Suicide Hill, then he'll ride
down Suicide Hill. . . ."

But Marvin never said he'd ride down Suicide Hill, thought Marvin.

"When?" demanded Clarence.

"Saturday," said Nick. "At twelve o' clock."

"High noon," said Stuart.

"This I've got to see," said Clarence.

"I'm going to get a front-row seat," said Travis.

"It's going to be the biggest wipe-out in history," said Clarence.

Read All the Marvin Redpost Books

More Books by Louis Sachar

MARVIN REDPOST
Super Fast, Out of Control!

LOUIS SACHAR
Illustrated by Adam Record

A STEPPING STONE BOOK™

Random House New York

Text copyright © 2000 by Louis Sachar
Cover art and interior illustrations copyright © 2015 by Adam Record

All rights reserved. Published in the United States by Random House Children's Books, a division of Penguin Random House LLC, New York. Previously published in the United States in paperback by Random House Children's Books, New York, in 2000.

Random House and the colophon are registered trademarks and A Stepping Stone Book and the colophon are trademarks of Penguin Random House LLC.

Visit us on the Web!
SteppingStonesBooks.com
randomhousekids.com

Educators and librarians, for a variety of teaching tools, visit us at
RHTeachersLibrarians.com

Library of Congress Cataloging-in-Publication Data
Sachar, Louis.
Marvin Redpost : super fast, out of control! / by Louis Sachar ; illustrated by Adam Record.
p. cm. A stepping stone book.
Summary: Afraid of his new mountain bike, third-grader Marvin finds himself in a desperate situation when he accepts a challenge to ride down Suicide Hill.
ISBN 978-0-679-89001-0 (trade) — ISBN 978-0-553-53545-7 (lib. bdg.) — ISBN 978-0-307-80574-4 (ebook)
[1. Bicycles and bicycling—Fiction. 2. Fear—Fiction.] I. Title.
PZ7.S1185Maq 2000 [Fic]—dc21 98-31276

Printed in the United States of America

38

This book has been officially leveled by using the F&P Text Level Gradient™ Leveling System.

To Carla

CONTENTS

1
Saturday

Marvin and his friends were hanging out in his backyard.

"What do you want to do?" asked Stuart.

"I dunno," said Marvin.

"It's no fair that your mom won't let us watch TV," griped Nick. "What's so special about fresh air?"

"Let's play unicorns," said Linzy. Linzy was Marvin's five-year-old sister.

"We're not playing unicorns," Marvin grumbled.

"So what do you want to do?" asked Stuart.

"I dunno," said Marvin.

"What about a video game?" asked Nick. "Does that count as TV?"

"I'm the gold unicorn," said Linzy. "Marvin's the rainbow unicorn. Nick, you can be the blue unicorn. Stuart will be the pink unicorn."

"I don't want to be pink," said Stuart. "Why can't I be the gold unicorn?"

"You can't start out being gold," Linzy explained. "First you have to do some good magic. Then the unicorn fairy will turn you into gold."

"We're not playing unicorns," said Marvin.

"How did *you* get to be gold?" asked Stuart.

"The unicorn fairy made me gold," said Linzy, "because I used my magic to save the princess."

"We're not playing unicorns," said Marvin.

"How do you play?" asked Nick.

Linzy stared at Nick. She had never heard such a dumb question in all her life. "You just pretend you're a unicorn," she said.

"How?" asked Stuart.

Linzy sighed. She couldn't believe Marvin had such stupid friends.

"Just pretend you're a magical horse with a horn in your head, like this."

She pranced around the yard, flapping her arms, and sang, *"I'm a unicorn. Yes, I am. I'm a gold unicorn. Yes, I am. Oh, I'm a gold unicorn. Yes, I am."*

Linzy stopped prancing and flapping. "Your turn, Marvin," she said.

"I don't want to," said Marvin.

"You have to. It's the rules," said Linzy.

"Except when I did it, I was gold. You have to be rainbow."

"Just get out of here, Linzy!" snapped Marvin. "Can't you see we're busy! You're such a stupid pest."

Linzy stared hard at Marvin. He was afraid she was going to cry.

"I'm telling the unicorn fairy on you!" she shouted, then stormed into the house. She slammed the door behind her.

Marvin sighed.

"So what do you want to do?" asked Stuart.

"I dunno," said Marvin.

"It's unfair your mom won't let us watch TV," said Nick. "What's wrong with her?"

Marvin shrugged.

"We could ride bikes," suggested Stuart.

Marvin got an uneasy feeling in his stomach. "There's nowhere to go," he said.

"Hey, didn't you get a new mountain bike?" asked Nick.

Marvin felt sick.

"That's right!" said Stuart. "How come you haven't shown it to us?"

Marvin shrugged. "It's just a bike."

"I know!" said Nick. "Let's ride our bikes down Suicide Hill!"

Just hearing those words made Marvin feel like he was falling down a very steep cliff.

Let's
  ride
    our
      bikes
        down
          SUICIDE HILL!!!!!!!

"I'll go home and get my bike," said Stuart. Marvin couldn't believe it. Nick was a daredevil, but he thought Stuart was smarter than that.

"I'll bring my stopwatch," said Nick. "Maybe we can break the record."

"Cool," said Stuart.

Marvin didn't care about breaking records. He was more worried about breaking bones.

Linzy returned to the back door. Marvin was glad to see her. He thought it might be fun to play unicorns after all.

"Mom wants to see you," Linzy said.

As Marvin walked into the house, Linzy said, "You're in big trouble now, mister."

They walked to their mother's office.

Marvin's mother was sitting at her desk, in front of the computer. She worked as an accountant. She helped people figure their taxes. She normally didn't work on Saturdays, but it was getting close to April 15, so she had been very busy lately.

"Did you yell at your sister?" she asked Marvin.

"Kind of," he admitted.

"You need to tell her you're sorry," said his mother.

Marvin turned to Linzy. She was wearing her sad and pitiful face.

He got an idea. "Why should I?" he asked boldly.

"I beg your pardon?" said his mother.

"Linzy is a pest," Marvin said.

"Marvin!" exclaimed his mother.

"Now he owes me two sorry's!" said Linzy.

"You're the one who should be sorry," said Marvin. "For being so stupid!"

Marvin's mother looked at him for a long moment. She didn't yell at him. She simply said, "You need to tell Nick and Stuart it's time for them to go home. Then you will spend the rest of the afternoon in your room."

Marvin pushed his luck. "That's not fair!" he exclaimed. "We were going to ride our bikes down Suicide Hill!"

"You won't be riding your bike for a week," said his mother.

Marvin went back outside and told his friends the bad news.

"Why? What did you do?" asked Stuart.

"Nothing," said Marvin. "My mom's just in a bad mood."

He told them good-bye, then went up to his room. He felt awful. He was glad he wouldn't have to ride down Suicide Hill, but he felt bad for calling Linzy a stupid pest. More than that, he felt terrible for being so afraid.

He wasn't just afraid of Suicide Hill. He was afraid to ride his new bike.

It seemed so big. And it had hand brakes.

He had never used hand brakes before. He also didn't know how to use all the different gears.

What made it worse, he was the one who had asked for a new bike. He'd begged for a new bike. His parents had said it was very expensive. They said he already had a bicycle, but he'd called that a "baby bike." He wanted a mountain bike. He said Linzy could have his old bike.

And in the end, they bought it for him.

That was ten days ago, and he still hadn't ridden it. Just thinking about it made him sick to his stomach.

At least he wouldn't have to ride it for a week. He wished he still had his baby bike.

2
Monday

"You're so brave," said Casey Happleton. She sat next to Marvin in Mrs. North's class. She had a ponytail that stuck out the side of her head, instead of the back.

Marvin shrugged and smiled. He didn't know why Casey thought he was brave, but he was glad she did.

"Judy and I are going to come watch you," said Casey.

"Watch me what? When?"

"Saturday," said Casey. "When you ride your new mountain bike down Suicide Hill."

Marvin felt as if he'd been kicked in the stomach. He tried not to show it. He didn't want Casey Happleton to think he was scared. "Who told you that?" he asked.

"Judy," said Casey. "She said you would have ridden down last Saturday, but you got in trouble for calling your sister a stupid pest. Now you can't ride your bike for a week."

Marvin didn't know how Judy Jasper knew so much about his life.

"Stuart told her," said Casey.

Marvin never told Stuart he'd ride down Suicide Hill on Saturday. He just told him that he couldn't ride his bike for a week.

"Marvin," said Mrs. North. "Have you been listening to anything I said?"

He looked at his teacher. "Um, I'm not sure. What did you say?"

Mrs. North gave Marvin The Look.

At recess, Marvin asked Stuart why he told Judy that he had called his sister a stupid pest.

"She asked me," said Stuart.

They were playing wizzle-fish tag.

"Let me get this straight," said Marvin. "Judy Jasper just came up to you and said, 'Did Marvin call his sister a stupid pest?'"

"Something like that," said Stuart.

"And you told her we're going to ride our bikes down Suicide Hill on Saturday?" Marvin asked.

"No," said Stuart.

Marvin was glad about that.

"I told her *you* were going to ride *your* bike down Suicide Hill. My mom won't let me."

"My mom won't let me, either," complained Nick. "Just because it's *dangerous* or something."

"But we'll come watch you," said Stuart.

"You might need someone to call 911," said Nick.

Marvin couldn't believe it. They were the ones who had wanted to ride down Suicide Hill, not him. He thought he remembered Nick bragging about how he'd ridden down Suicide Hill lots of times, full speed all the way.

"I thought you said you've ridden down Suicide Hill," he said.

"No, I never said that," said Nick.

Marvin knew he was lying.

He tossed a paper plate on the ground and

stepped on it. Everyone had two paper plates. The paper plates were the wizzle fish.

Clarence and Travis wizzled beside him.

"Hey, Marvin," said Clarence. "Are you really going to ride down Suicide Hill?"

"Uh, I'm not sure."

"See, I told you he was chicken!" Clarence told Travis.

"We're not scared," said Nick.

We? thought Marvin.

"If Marvin says he'll ride down Suicide Hill, then he'll ride down Suicide Hill," said Stuart. He patted Marvin on the back.

But Marvin never said he'd ride down Suicide Hill, thought Marvin.

"When?" demanded Clarence.

"Saturday," said Nick. "At twelve o'clock."

"High noon," said Stuart.

"This I've got to see," said Clarence.

"I'm going to get a front-row seat," said Travis.

"It's going to be the biggest wipe-out in history," said Clarence. He and Travis laughed.

Marvin didn't know what to do. Everything was happening too fast. He felt like he was speeding downhill, out of control, unable to stop. He wanted to scream.

3
Tuesday

Linzy was wearing unicorn pajamas. "Do you want to frolic?" she asked.

"Frolic?" asked Marvin. He didn't know what the word meant. He wasn't sure it was a real word.

"That's what unicorns do," Linzy explained. "We frolic."

She showed Marvin how to frolic. She skipped down the hall and sang, *"We're happy, happy unicorns. Oh, happy unicorns frolicking."*

Marvin didn't feel like frolicking. He wasn't a happy unicorn.

It was Tuesday night. Saturday was only four days away.

He could see the light on in his brother's room. Jacob was doing homework. Jacob had ridden down Suicide Hill before.

Marvin knocked on his brother's door.

"What?"

Jacob sounded annoyed. They gave a lot of homework in middle school.

"I just wanted to ask you something," Marvin said timidly.

"What?" asked Jacob.

Marvin wasn't sure what to ask. "I don't remember," he said.

Jacob glared at him.

Marvin could tell Jacob thought he was just a dumb little kid. Marvin felt like a dumb little kid.

He headed back to his room.

The whole school was expecting him to ride down Suicide Hill on Saturday. He couldn't figure out how it happened. He never wanted to ride down Suicide Hill in the first place. It was Stuart and Nick's idea, but their parents wouldn't let them.

That gave him an idea. It was so obvious, he wondered why he hadn't thought of it sooner. He walked quickly to his mother's office.

His mother was working on the computer. She turned and smiled at Marvin as he entered.

"Sorry to bother you," Marvin said.

"Oh, that's okay." She took a sip of coffee.

"In four days I get to ride my bike," Marvin said.

"That's right," said his mother. "I hope you've learned your lesson."

Marvin nodded. "You know the first place

I'm going to ride it?" he asked, trying to sound excited.

His mother smiled and asked, "Where?"

"Suicide Hill!"

"Sounds exciting," said his mother. She entered some numbers into the computer.

Marvin thought maybe she hadn't heard him. Or maybe she thought it was no big deal, since Jacob had ridden down it lots of times. Didn't she realize Jacob was a lot older?

"*Suicide* Hill," he repeated. "I'm going to ride my brand-new expensive bike super fast down Suicide Hill!"

"I'm glad to see you're so excited about riding your new bike. Your father and I were beginning to wonder."

"Stuart's and Nick's parents won't let them ride their bikes down Suicide Hill," said Marvin.

"I guess they think it's dangerous or something. For a *third grader.*"

"I guess," said his mother. She entered some more numbers into the computer.

Marvin wondered if she heard anything he said. He kept trying. "I guess Stuart's mom is worried he might break his arm, or worse."

"I know you'll be careful," said his mother.

"Sure, I'll try to be careful," said Marvin. "But when you're going downhill super fast, out of control, it's—"

"Is it raining?" asked his mother.

Marvin didn't know what that had to do with anything. "I don't think so," he said, but then he saw a flash of lightning.

A few seconds later, he heard thunder. A few seconds after that, Linzy came running into the room.

"Turn off the computer!" she screamed. She was wearing her wild and worried face. She clutched her mother.

"There's nothing to worry about," said her mother.

There was another flash of lightning. "Turn it off! Turn it off!" Linzy demanded. She was crying.

"I know you're scared," said her mother. "But I—"

"The lightning will come through the computer!" Linzy shrieked.

Her mother sighed. "We are all very safe," she said.

Marvin's father came into the study. He picked up Linzy and held her close. "Everything is all right," he told her.

"She has to turn it off before it explodes."

"She has an important job to do. And it's our job to let her do it. You too, Marvin."

Marvin followed his father as he carried Linzy to her room and set her on her bed.

"Can I sleep with you, Marvin?" Linzy asked. "Please?"

Marvin felt bad for her, but he'd tried sleeping with Linzy once before. She could never keep still. She kept kicking him all night, and ended up sleeping sideways across the bed.

"Lightning and thunder are just part of nature," he said.

"The bad part," said Linzy.

"You are perfectly safe," said her father. "Do you think I would leave you alone if I thought you were in danger?"

"No," Linzy whimpered.

"You're the gold unicorn," said Marvin. "Unicorns aren't afraid of storms."

There was a loud clap of thunder, and she ducked under the covers.

"You know the thunder can't hurt you," said her father.

"I know," Linzy said, from under the covers.

"But you're still scared?" asked her father.

"Yes."

"Try to be brave," said her father. "Remember, the fear isn't on the outside. The fear is inside your head."

Linzy's head came out from under the covers. She looked puzzled, as if she was trying to figure out what that meant.

Marvin tried to figure it out, too.

"You need to stand up to that storm," said her father. "And say, 'I'm not afraid of you!'"

Linzy gave it a try. She sat up straight in her bed and looked out the window. "I'm not afraid of you!" she declared.

"Good," said her father. "That's my brave girl." He kissed her good night, then started out the door. "C'mon, Marvin."

Marvin could see Linzy trembling with fear. As he walked out the door, he heard her whisper to herself, "I'm a gold unicorn. Yes, I am. Oh, I'm a very brave unicorn. Yes, I am."

4
Wednesday

Marvin knew what he had to do. He just had to stand up to Suicide Hill and say, "I'm not afraid of you!"

It was like his father had said. The fear was all inside his head. There was nothing on the outside that was scary. His mother would never let him ride down Suicide Hill if it was really dangerous. Would she?

Jacob had gone down Suicide Hill lots of times. If Jacob could do it, so could he.

"Keep your tongue inside your mouth," said Casey Happleton.

Marvin was eating lunch. He thought his tongue *was* inside his mouth.

"My brother's friend knows someone who bit off the tip of his tongue while riding down Suicide Hill," said Casey.

Marvin touched the tip of his tongue to his teeth.

"It wasn't even a wipe-out," said Casey. "He was going down Suicide Hill real fast, and the tip of his tongue was sticking out of his mouth, like this."

Casey held her fists out in front of her, like she was gripping handlebars. She looked like she was concentrating really hard. Her tongue stuck out of her mouth.

Everybody else at the table laughed, but Marvin didn't see anything funny about it.

"Then his bike hit just a tiny little itty-bitty rock," said Casey, "and he bit it off. He didn't even know he did it until he got to the bottom of the hill and tried to talk."

Casey did an impersonation of someone trying to talk without a tongue. Again, everyone except Marvin laughed.

"What happened to his tongue?" asked Stuart.

"No one knows," said Casey. "They had a whole huge search party out to look for it, but no one ever found it. It's still up there, somewhere."

"Maybe Marvin will find it," said Judy.

Marvin shrugged. His mouth was closed tight. His tongue was safely on the inside.

"Be sure your shoelaces are tied real good," warned Kenny. "My cousin knows someone whose shoelace got wrapped around his bike pedal. He was riding his bike real fast, and

every time the pedal went around, it made his
shoe tighter . . . and tighter . . . and tighter . . .
and tighter . . . and tighter. There was nothing
he could do. He was going too fast to stop."

"What happened?" asked Nick.

"It strangled his foot. He lost two toes."

"How?" asked Casey. "What'd they do, pop off his foot?"

"I don't know how it happened," said Kenny. "I wasn't there. Somebody told my cousin about it, and my cousin doesn't lie."

"Which toes did he lose?" asked Judy.

"The thumb-toe and the pinky-toe, I think. He still has his three middle ones."

"They're not called the thumb-toe and pinky-toe," said Stuart. "It's big toe and little toe."

"My thumb-toe isn't my biggest toe," said Melanie. "My second toe is bigger than my thumb-toe."

"My toes are different on each foot," said Judy Jasper.

Judy took off her shoes and socks. She explained that her parents' feet were different. On her mother's feet, the thumb-toe was the biggest. On her father's feet, the second toe was the biggest.

Judy showed everyone her feet. On her left

foot, her thumb-toe was the biggest. On her right foot, the second toe was the biggest. "I call this one my mommy foot, and this one my daddy foot," she said.

Nick stared at Judy's feet. "That's the most amazing thing I've ever seen in my whole life," he said.

Marvin didn't even look at Judy's amazing feet. He was thinking about how often his shoelaces came untied, even when they were double-knotted.

The lunch teacher, Mrs. Grant, came by and made Judy put her shoes and socks back on.

5
Thursday

A policewoman came to Marvin's classroom. She wore a blue police uniform and a silver badge. Handcuffs dangled from her belt. She didn't have a gun. Her hair was red, like Marvin's, and almost as short.

"This is Officer Watson," said Mrs. North. "She wants to talk to us about something important, and she's also brought some interesting things to share with us."

Marvin wondered if she was there to tell him

not to ride down Suicide Hill. He hoped so.

Officer Watson said hello to the class. The first thing she showed them was a bulletproof vest. She put it on over her police uniform. Then she took it off and passed it around the room.

Marvin was surprised by how heavy it was. Officer Watson must be really strong, he realized, to wear it. He wished he could borrow it when he rode down Suicide Hill. *If* he rode down Suicide Hill.

"Are those real handcuffs?" asked Nick.

Officer Watson turned to Mrs. North and asked, "Aren't they supposed to raise their hands before asking a question?"

"They're supposed to," said Mrs. North.

Officer Watson wiggled her finger at Nick, asking for him to come up to the front of the room.

Marvin watched Nick nervously get out of his chair and go to her.

"Hold out your hand," she told him.

Nick held out his hand.

Officer Watson took the handcuffs off her belt. She clasped one of the cuffs around Nick's wrist.

Everyone laughed.

Then she walked him over to Mrs. North. She clasped the other cuff around Mrs. North's wrist.

Marvin gasped. Next to him, Casey Happleton laughed so hard her ponytail went around in circles.

"Yes, those are real handcuffs," Officer Watson told Nick.

Marvin had never seen Nick's face so red.

Officer Watson patted her pockets. "What did I do with the key?" she asked. She looked worried.

So did Nick.

But she was only kidding. She unlocked the
handcuffs, and Nick ran back to his seat.

She also brought a fingerprint kit. She had
everyone press their thumbs on an ink pad and
put their thumbprints on a piece of paper.

The whole class had purple thumbs.

The last thing Officer Watson showed them was a lie detector.

"I bet Mrs. North would love to have that!" said Travis.

"I don't need one," said Mrs. North. "I always know when one of my students isn't telling the truth. That's the first thing you learn when you become a teacher."

"Who would like to try it out?" asked Officer Watson.

Marvin had an awful feeling in the pit of his stomach. He *knew* Officer Watson was going to call on him and ask him if he was scared to ride his bike.

He ducked his head down and tried to hide behind Warren, the boy who sat in front of him. He felt like a criminal.

Officer Watson seemed to be looking right at him. "How about you?" she asked.

"Okay," said Casey Happleton. She hopped out of her seat. Marvin watched her sideways ponytail bob up and down as she went to the front of the room.

The lie detector was on Mrs. North's desk. Casey sat in Mrs. North's chair. Officer Watson attached some wires to Casey's right arm and fingers. She strapped a belt around her chest.

"I'm going to ask you some questions," Officer Watson told Casey. "This machine will let me know if you are lying. Ready?"

"Ready," said Casey.

"What's your name?"

"Michael Jordan," said Casey.

Officer Watson checked the machine. "That was not the truth," she said.

41

"Casey Happleton," said Casey.

"How old are you?"

"Nine."

"What did you have for breakfast this morning?"

"Scrambled eggs."

"I don't think that's the truth," said Officer Watson.

Casey sighed. "Well, my mom gave me scrambled eggs, but I fed them to my dog."

"How does that machine know what Casey had for breakfast?" asked Clarence.

"It doesn't," said Officer Watson. "When you tell a lie, your body gets nervous. Your muscles tense. You sweat a little bit more, and there are changes in your heartbeat and breathing. The machine registers those changes in your body."

She asked Casey some more questions.

"Did you do all your homework yesterday?"

"Yes."

"Did anyone help you?"

"No."

Officer Watson cleared her throat. "Are you sure?"

Casey frowned. "My mom helped me."

"That's better," said Officer Watson.

"There's nothing wrong with that," said Mrs. North.

"Do you like Mrs. North?" asked Officer Watson.

"Hey!" Casey exclaimed. "That's not a fair question."

"Okay, I'll ask a different question."

"Ask her if she likes Marvin Redpost!" called Melanie.

Officer Watson smiled. "Who's Marvin Redpost?"

Everyone pointed at Marvin.

Officer Watson turned back to Casey. "Do you like Marvin Redpost?"

Marvin buried his head under his arms. But he didn't cover his ears. For a long time Casey didn't answer. Then she said, "I like Mrs. North."

Officer Watson unhooked her and let her return to her seat.

"Okay, we've had some fun," Officer Watson told the class. "But now I want everyone to settle down. I want to talk to you about something important. It may save your life."

Marvin paid close attention.

"I'm talking about illegal drugs," said Officer Watson.

She told the class that drugs were bad for them. Drugs could kill you. Drugs could destroy your brain and make you stupid. If you started doing drugs, even just once, you might not be able to stop.

Everybody promised Officer Watson they would never take illegal drugs.

She walked around the room and in between the desks. She stopped next to Kenny. "What if all your friends took drugs?" she asked him. "Then would you?"

"No way!" said Kenny.

She turned to Nick. "What if they said they wouldn't be your friends unless you took drugs?"

"Then they're not really my friends," said Nick.

"If my friend jumped off the Empire State Building, that doesn't mean I should jump off, too," said Judy.

"If they were my friends," said Casey Happleton, "I would do everything I could to get them to stop using drugs."

"Very good," said Officer Watson. She leaned on Marvin's desk and stared right into his eyes. "What about you, Marvin?" she asked. "What if everyone said, 'Marvin Redpost is chicken!'?"

She made him feel nervous. "I—I still w-wouldn't," he said.

"Good for you," she said. "That's not being scared. That's being smart. Remember, taking drugs doesn't make you brave. It takes a lot more courage, sometimes, to say no to your friends."

Marvin nodded. His hands were sweaty. His body was tense. His heart was beating a little faster than normal. He took a deep breath.

6
Still Only Thursday

Marvin sat on a stool in the kitchen. He stared at the wall. He'd been sitting that way ever since he got home from school.

He didn't know what he was supposed to do. Should he look his fear in the eye and ride down Suicide Hill? Or was that stupid, like taking drugs? Officer Watson had said that sometimes the bravest thing you can do is say no to your friends.

He knew his friends wouldn't think he was being brave. They'd think he was scared.

And they'd be right. He was scared of Suicide Hill. But maybe he was smart to be scared.

His father had told Linzy she had to stand up to her fears. But Suicide Hill was different than thunder and lightning. He could get hurt going down Suicide Hill. Thunder and lightning couldn't hurt Linzy.

No, that wasn't true either, he realized. Maybe thunder couldn't hurt her, but if she got struck by lightning, it could kill her. Maybe Linzy was right. Maybe lightning could come through the computer.

Going down Suicide Hill wasn't as bad as being struck by lightning. He didn't think he'd be killed going down Suicide Hill. Maybe just break an arm and a leg.

Other kids have ridden down Suicide Hill,

he reminded himself. *They didn't get hurt.*

So? Other kids have taken drugs, too. Just because other kids do something, that doesn't mean you should, too. If your friends jump off the Empire State Building, that doesn't mean you should, too.

But Nick and Stuart weren't even jumping off the Empire State Building. They just expected him to jump.

Maybe his friends had forgotten all about Suicide Hill. Nobody mentioned it once today at school. All anyone talked about was Officer Watson and the lie detector.

He never felt more confused in his life. He wished he could practice riding his bike. He needed to see how the brakes and gears worked.

He remembered the man at the bike shop telling him never to use just the front brake. He was supposed to use the back brake, or both brakes together. If he tried to stop using just the front brake, the bike might flip over on his head.

The front door opened. "Hey, Mar," said Jacob.

"Hiya, Marvin," said Nate. Nate was Jacob's best friend.

They threw their backpacks on the counter and attacked the refrigerator.

"I hear you're going to ride down Suicide Hill," said Nate.

"Uh, maybe," said Marvin.

"You better not wimp out," said Nate. "Some of the guys at school said you were a baby, but I stuck up for you. Now my reputation is on the line."

Marvin didn't say anything. He couldn't believe middle school kids had been talking about him, a puny third grader.

"Can I ask you a question?" he asked his brother.

50

"Sure," said Jacob, his mouth full of cookies and pickles.

"How do you know which is front and which is back?"

"What?" asked Jacob.

"Well, I haven't really ridden my bike a whole lot. How do you know which brake is for the front tire, and which one is for the back tire?"

Jacob thought a moment as he swallowed a mouthful of food. "Right is back, left is front," he said. "No, wait. Right is front, left is back. No, I think I was right the first time. Left is front—"

"Left is back, right is front," said Nate.

"No, right is back, left is front," said Jacob.

"You sure?" asked Nate.

"I think so," said Jacob.

It always took Marvin a moment to figure out his left from his right. He knew he wouldn't have time if he was speeding down Suicide Hill.

"I really don't think about it when I'm on my bike," said Nate. "It just comes natural."

"You don't want to brake just with your front brake," said Jacob. "Your bike could flip over."

Marvin nodded. He'd heard that before.

"Suicide Hill is so steep, you should probably use both brakes all the time," said Nate.

"What about gears?" Marvin asked.

"What about them?" asked Nate.

"Do I need to shift gears? Which gear should I use?"

"High gear," said Jacob.

"Low gear," said Nate, at almost the same time.

"Low gear going up, high gear going down," said Jacob.

"I thought it was high gear going up, and low gear going down," said Nate.

"No, low up, high down," said Jacob.

"I don't really think about it when I'm on my bike," said Nate. "It just comes natural."

Marvin didn't think it would come natural to him.

"You won't need to worry about gears going down the hill," said Jacob. "You'll coast almost the whole way. But remember to lean into the turns."

Marvin didn't know what that meant.

"You have to lean your bike way over on the sharp turns," Nate explained. "Have you ever watched a motorcycle race? They lean way over the whole time."

Marvin had never seen a motorcycle race. He didn't want to do any fancy riding. He just wanted to get down the hill alive. "I'm just going to try to keep my bike straight up," he said.

"You can't do that," said Jacob. "You have to

lean into the turns. Otherwise you'll slide off the path and you'll go over the cliff."

"It comes natural," Nate assured him.

Jacob and Nate went on up to Jacob's room.

Marvin stayed where he was, staring at the wall. *Well, it's only Thursday,* he told himself.

He still had two whole days.

7
Saturday

Marvin couldn't believe it was already Saturday. What happened to Friday? The week had sped by super fast, out of control.

He walked out through the laundry room into the garage. His shoes were double-knotted. So was his stomach.

His bike was leaning against the side wall. It had been leaning there for almost three weeks. "Don't you want to try it out?" his father had asked when they first brought it home from the bike shop.

"I'm kind of tired," Marvin had said.

Now he took hold of the handlebars. "I'm not afraid of you," he whispered. He slowly rolled the bike backward, between the van and the garbage pail. The pedal banged against his shin as he made his way out of the garage and onto the driveway.

He still hadn't decided if he would go down Suicide Hill, but he had to go at least as far as Stuart's house. It was decided that he and Nick would meet at Stuart's, and then they'd all ride to Suicide Hill together.

Nick and Stuart were the ones who decided this. It seemed to Marvin that he didn't make any of his own decisions anymore. His life was being decided by others.

His bike helmet dangled off the end of one handlebar. He put it on, but it didn't seem to fit right. The strap was too tight under his chin, and the helmet seemed way too loose at the top of his head. He hoped he hadn't put it on backward.

He stared at his giant bicycle. His parents had chosen a bicycle that was a little big for him. "You'll grow into it," his father had said. "We don't want to have to buy another bike in six months."

He had to lean it way over to try and get his leg over it. It was impossible. As he tried to lift himself onto the seat, the bike almost fell. He just managed to stick his foot out and catch himself.

He tried several more times, hopping on one foot and scraping his leg against the pedal. He couldn't do it.

How am I supposed to ride down Suicide Hill if I can't even get on my bike? he wondered.

He thought about all the kids waiting for him at Suicide Hill. Casey and Judy. Clarence and Travis. Nate and all the kids from middle school.

Marvin walked the bike down the driveway and into the street. He edged it next to the curb and then rotated the pedals into position. Then, standing on the curb, he was able to stretch his leg over the top of the bike and just barely touch the pedal on the other side.

He hopped on. The bike wobbled. The tire rubbed against the curb and he almost fell, but he managed to turn the handlebars and straighten out. He pedaled hard. He felt himself gain his balance. He headed toward Stuart's house.

Now that Marvin was on the bike, it felt almost the same as his old bike. He was just higher off the ground. He didn't try to shift gears. And he hoped he wouldn't have to use the brakes.

There was only one corner between his house and Stuart's. He took it nice and slow, almost too slow. He found it easier to keep his balance when he was going a little faster, but if he went too fast, he might have to use his brakes.

Stuart's driveway was uphill. It slowed him down enough that he didn't have to use his brakes. He let the bike roll to a stop, then hopped off. He let it fall beside him.

He knocked on Stuart's door. As he waited for someone to answer it, he looked back at his bike. He hoped he'd be able to get back on it without too much trouble.

Stuart's mother opened the door and said, "Hi, Marvin. Come on in. The boys are watching a movie."

Marvin walked through the kitchen and into

the family room. His friends were lying on the floor, staring at the TV. Before he could say anything, Nick said, "Shush! It's the good part."

"It's almost twelve o'clock," said Marvin. "We have to get going."

"After the movie," said Stuart.

Marvin couldn't believe it. "How long will that be?" he asked.

"I don't know," said Stuart.

"Shush!" said Nick.

"Can't you watch it later?" Marvin asked.

"You look funny in that helmet," said Stuart.

"Do you think it's on backward?" Marvin asked.

Stuart didn't answer. He was staring back at the TV set.

"It's a video," Marvin pointed out. "You can watch it later."

"We want to watch it now," said Nick. "Besides, we haven't had lunch yet."

"Lunch!" exclaimed Marvin. "Everyone is waiting for me at Suicide Hill."

"Then go," said Stuart. "I still have to eat lunch."

"Ooh, did you see that?" asked Nick.

"Gross!" said Stuart.

Marvin didn't know what to do. He didn't want to have to go to Suicide Hill alone. He didn't even know if he was allowed to ride there alone.

He was allowed to ride to Stuart's house, because it was just around the block. Suicide Hill was much farther away.

He decided to call home. If his mother wouldn't let him go, then there was nothing he could do about it. No one could blame him. It would be her fault. And Stuart and Nick's.

He used the kitchen phone. His father was the one who answered. Marvin explained the problem.

"I think it will be fine," his father said. "There are no busy streets along the way. And I appreciate the fact that you called. It shows you're responsible. If you didn't call, I wouldn't have let you go."

Marvin hung up. He tried to make sense of

what his father said. If he didn't call, how could his father have said he couldn't go?

He wished he'd talked to his mother instead. She never would have let him go.

"Well, I'm going," he told Nick and Stuart. "So long."

They stared at the TV.

He went back outside. He picked up his bike and walked it down the driveway.

He wasn't sure he'd ride down Suicide Hill, but at least he had to go there. He couldn't leave everybody waiting. He had to be brave enough to tell them he was scared.

He set his bike next to the curb. He put his foot on the pedal and quickly hoisted his other leg over. He was up and pedaling before he had time to worry about it.

He rode quickly, afraid that he was already late. He turned right off Stuart's street, rode past two more streets, then turned left on the road that led to Suicide Hill.

The road was uphill the whole way. It became harder and harder to pedal. He wondered if he should try shifting gears.

He had two gear shifts, one on either end of his handlebars. The one on his left was numbered **1** to **3**. The arrow was in the middle, at **2**. The one on his right was numbered **1** to **7**. The arrow pointed to **5**. He took a chance. He rotated the right gear shift one notch, so that the arrow pointed to **6**.

Suddenly it became almost impossible to pedal. His bike slowed to a stop, and he had to put his foot down to keep from falling.

He caught his breath. He knew he should never have tried shifting gears. He promised himself never to do that again.

He walked his bike to the curb and hopped

back on. But once again, he couldn't pedal, and he fell off to the side.

It was impossible. The bike was in the wrong gear, and he couldn't shift gears until the bike was moving. But how could he get it moving if it was in the wrong gear?

He wondered if the kids at Suicide Hill were getting impatient. He could imagine some of the middle schoolers telling Nate, "See, I told you Marvin Redpost was a wimp."

He turned the bike around and pointed it downhill. He didn't bother taking it to the curb. He just stepped on the pedal and threw his other leg over as he rolled down the hill.

The bike wasn't really *that* big.

He shifted the gear back to **5.** Then he shifted one notch further, to **4.**

He made a U-turn and continued up the hill. It was a lot easier to pedal now that he was in a lower gear. He shifted to **3**. Even better.

He had to keep on shifting gears as he continued following the road higher and higher. After a while both gears were pointed at **1**, and it was still hard to pedal.

Ahead of him, the road made a sharp turn to the left. A steel barrier prevented cars from going straight.

But Marvin wasn't in a car. Using his right-hand brake, he stopped his bike. He got off and walked around the barrier. He took several long, deep breaths, then looked over the edge of Suicide Hill.

8
The Hill

Where was everybody? Marvin wondered if maybe they all got tired of waiting and went home. Or they could be waiting at the bottom of the hill. After all, why should *they* struggle to get to the top?

"Hello!" he shouted. "I'm here!"

There was no answer.

He couldn't see the bottom of the hill. His eyes followed a dirt path that zigzagged through some rocks, then disappeared behind a large bush. He couldn't see anything beyond that.

"Anyone down there?" he called.

A van stopped on the other side of the barrier. Marvin turned around to see his mother. She got out of the van and stepped over the barrier. "Since Nick and Stuart weren't riding with you, I thought I'd better make sure you were all right."

Marvin was glad to see her.

"I dropped Jacob, Linzy, and your dad at the bottom of the hill," she said. "They wanted to see you come down."

"Was anyone else there?" asked Marvin.

"No."

"You sure?" Marvin asked.

"I didn't see anybody."

"Do you know what time it is?"

His mother checked her watch. "A couple of minutes after twelve."

"What about Nate?" Marvin asked. "Did he come with Jacob?"

"No."

Marvin couldn't believe it. Although, now that he thought about it, Nate had never said he was coming. And none of Marvin's classmates had talked about Suicide Hill since that day at lunch. When was that? Wednesday? Three days ago.

He shook his head and smiled. He had been so worried about what everybody else thought. But nobody else really cared.

"So *this* is Suicide Hill," said his mother, peering over the edge.

Marvin nodded.

"It's steep, isn't it?"

Marvin nodded again.

"You sure this is something you want to

do?" she asked. "You don't have to if you don't want to."

"I know," said Marvin.

He looked back down the hill. He wrapped his fingers around the handlebars. The bike felt sturdy. Not like his old baby bike. This bike was made for this hill.

"I want to," he said.

It felt good to make his own decision. Not for anyone else. For himself.

He looked back down the hill and whispered, "Oh, I'm a very brave unicorn. Yes, I am." Then he stepped up on the pedal and swung his leg over the other side.

He shifted the gears as he watched the front tire slowly roll over the edge. The trail was narrow and steep. He squeezed both brakes as he tried to stay in the middle of the dirt path. He went between a couple of jagged boulders, then

around a large bush. His tires skidded from side to side.

At last he came to a place where the trail was straight, so he eased off the brakes. That was a mistake.

The next thing he knew, he was speeding toward a cliff. He gripped the brakes hard and turned sharply. The wheels skidded inches from the cliff. He had to jerk the bike back the other way to avoid a sharp-edged boulder—once again he was heading toward the cliff. Gripping the brakes with all his might, he leaned into the turn.

The trail then widened and got easier. He caught his breath. He came to a point where he went uphill for a short distance and needed to pedal. He shifted to a lower gear.

Then the trail turned back downhill. He went through a series of wide, smooth turns that were fast and fun.

It kind of looked like this.

As Marvin made the last turn, he could see the bottom of the hill. The rest of the way was very steep, but straight. Then it opened up into a wide, flat area. He let go of the brakes and went full speed.

As he streaked down the hill, he saw his family waving their arms and cheering for him. His father did one of his real loud whistles.

"Way to go, Mar!" Jacob called as Marvin went flying past him.

He made a U-turn and brought his bike to a halt next to Linzy.

"You're a gold unicorn now," she told him.

Marvin smiled. His heart was beating super fast, out of control.

9
Monday

Nobody asked Marvin about Suicide Hill. Marvin didn't tell anybody.

Only one person cared whether or not Marvin Redpost rode his bike down Suicide Hill. That person was Marvin Redpost.

Read on for a peek at

3
The Magic Crystal

"Do you want to know a secret?" asked Casey.

Marvin shrugged.

"Follow me," she said. "I'll tell you in the library." She started up the stairs.

Marvin followed. He was glad to be going to the library. Maybe he'd get to slide down the fire pole.

By the time he reached the fourth floor, his legs were sore and he was out of breath. He was not used to climbing so many stairs.

"In here," said Casey.

She opened the door to the library. The room was shaped like an octagon. Every wall was covered with bookshelves. The fire pole came up through the middle of the room. There was a railing around it, so somebody wouldn't accidentally fall through the hole.

"Do you know why you came to my house today?" Casey asked him.

"Um . . . no," said Marvin. He didn't want her to think he liked her.

"Because of this!" said Casey. She pulled something out of her pocket. "It's a magic crystal. It makes all your wishes come true." She showed it to Marvin.

Marvin took it from her and examined it. It was almost transparent, with flecks of green and gold.

"It used to be just a normal rock," Casey explained. "Then, last night, it got struck by lightning! And it turned into a magic crystal."

Marvin remembered that it had stormed last night. The lightning and thunder had scared his little sister, Linzy. But how would Casey know that the lightning had struck this rock?

"I wished that you'd come to my house today," said Casey. "And here you are."

Marvin knew that had nothing to do with the rock. The only reason he was here was because Stuart and Nick had gotten into a fight. "What other wishes have you made?" he asked.

"Just two other wishes so far," said Casey. "You have to be real careful with wishes. First I wished that Judy and I would be friends forever."

That doesn't prove anything, Marvin thought.

"And then," said Casey, "remember when

Clarence was bragging about how he can stick a needle through his finger?"

Marvin remembered. Clarence was grossing out everybody in class.

"I wished he'd be quiet," said Casey. "And he was!"

"Mrs. North told him to be quiet," Marvin pointed out.

"I wished it right before Mrs. North told him," said Casey.

Marvin didn't think that proved anything either.

"You try," said Casey.

Marvin looked at the rock.

"You have to close your eyes and squeeze the crystal as hard as you can, so that it hurts. Then make a wish," said Casey.

Marvin tried to think of something to wish for. He felt silly. He closed his eyes and squeezed

the rock so hard it hurt the palm of his hand. "I wish I knew when the book report was due."

"That doesn't count," said Casey. "I already told you it was due Tuesday. You have to make a *real* wish."

"Okay," Marvin said, glad that he finally knew when the report was due. He closed his eyes and squeezed the rock again. "I wish I had an ice cream sundae."

He opened his eyes.

No ice cream sundae.

Casey leaned over the railing and screamed down into the hole. "Dad! Marvin wants an ice cream sundae!"

Marvin leaned over the railing as well. He saw Casey's father way down at the bottom of the pole. It was a long way down. Marvin wasn't so sure he wanted to slide down it anymore. He felt a little dizzy.

"How many scoops?" Casey's father called up.

"How many scoops do you want, Marvin?" Casey asked him.

"Uh, two."

"We both want two scoops!" Casey shouted.

She turned back to Marvin. "My dad makes the best ice cream sundaes."

"Well, that doesn't count," said Marvin. "If your dad makes it."

"Why not?" asked Casey. "You wished for an ice cream sundae. And now you're going to get one."

Still, it seemed to Marvin he would have gotten the sundae even without the magic crystal. But now that he thought about it, he did wonder why he'd agreed to come to Casey's house.

"When did you wish for me to come over?" he asked her. "Before or after Stuart and Nick got in a fight?"

"Before," said Casey.

"That's weird," said Marvin. "I was supposed to go to Stuart's house today. The only reason I didn't was because he had to stay after school for fighting."

More terrific novels by
LOUIS SACHAR!

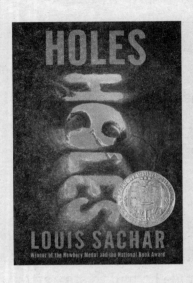

THE 33 STRATEGIES OF WAR

OTHER TITLES BY ROBERT GREENE

The Art of Seduction (A Joost Elffers Production)
The 48 Laws of Power (A Joost Elffers Production)

THE 33 STRATEGIES OF

W
A
R

CONCISE EDITION

ROBERT GREENE

A JOOST ELFFERS BOOK

P
PROFILE BOOKS

This concise edition published in Great Britain in 2008 by
PROFILE BOOKS LTD

3 Holford Yard
Bevin Way
London WC1X 9HD
www.profilebooks.com

Derived from *The 33 Strategies of War*, which was first published in Great Britain in 2006 by Profile Books and was first published in the United States in 2006 by Viking, a division of Penguin Putnam Inc.

Copyright © Robert Greene and Joost Elffers, 2006, 2007

A CIP catalogue record for this book is available from the British Library.

ISBN 978 1 86197 998 8

CONTENTS

PART

I

SELF-DIRECTED WARFARE

War, or any kind of conflict, is waged and won through strategy. Your mind is the starting point of all war and all strategy. A mind that is easily overwhelmed by emotion, that is rooted in the past instead of the present, that cannot see the world with clarity and urgency, will create strategies that will always miss the mark.

To become a true strategist, you must take three steps. First, become aware of the weakness and illness that can take hold of the mind, warping its strategic powers. Second, declare a kind of war on yourself to make yourself move forward. Third, wage ruthless and continual battle on the enemies within you by applying certain strategies.

The following four chapters are designed to make you aware of the disorders that are probably flourishing in your mind right now and to arm you with specific strategies for eliminating them.

1

DECLARE WAR ON YOUR ENEMIES
THE POLARITY STRATEGY

Life is endless battle and conflict, and you cannot fight effectively unless you can identify your enemies. People are subtle and evasive, disguising their intentions, pretending to be on your side. You need clarity. Learn to smoke out your enemies, to spot them by the signs and patterns that reveal hostility. Then, once you have them in your sights, inwardly declare war. As the opposite poles of a magnet create motion, your enemies—your opposites—can fill you with purpose and direction. As people who stand in your way, who represent what you loathe, people to react against, they are a source of energy. Do not be naïve: with some enemies there can be no compromise, no middle ground.

KEYS TO WARFARE

We live in an era in which people are seldom directly hostile. The rules of engagement—social, political, military—have changed, and so must your notion of the enemy. Although the world is more competitive than ever, outward aggression is discouraged, so people have learned to go underground, to attack unpredictably and craftily. Many use friendship as a way to mask aggressive desires: they come close to you to do more harm.

Your first task as a strategist is to widen your concept of the enemy, to include in that group those who are working against you, thwarting you, even in subtle ways. Do not be the naïve victim. Do not find yourself constantly retreating, reacting to your enemies' maneuvers. Arm yourself with prudence, and never completely lay down your arms, not even for friends.

People are usually good at hiding their hostility, but often they unconsciously give off signals showing that all is not what it seems. The point is not to mistrust all friendly gestures but to notice them. Register any change in the emotional temperature: unusual chumminess, a new desire to exchange confidences, excessive praise of you to third parties, the desire for an alliance that may make more sense for the other person than for you. Trust your instincts: if someone's behavior seems suspicious, it probably is.

You can sit back and read the signs or you can actively work to uncover your enemies—beat the grass to startle the snakes, as the Chinese say.

Do something that can be read in more than one way, that may be superficially polite but that could also indicate a slight coolness on your part or be seen as a subtle insult. A friend may wonder but will let it pass. The secret enemy, though, will react with anger. Any strong emotion and you will know that there's something boiling under the surface.

Understand: people tend to be vague and slippery because it is safer than outwardly committing to something. Beware of people who hide behind a façade of vague abstractions and impartiality: no one is impartial. A sharply worded question, an opinion designed to offend, will make them react and take sides.

Sometimes it is better to take a less direct approach with your potential enemies—to be as subtle and conniving as they are. If friends or followers whom you suspect of ulterior motives suggest something subtly hostile, or against your interests, go along, or seem to turn a blind eye: your enemies will soon go further, showing more of their hand. Now you have them in sight, and you can attack.

An enemy is often large and hard to pinpoint—an organization, or a person hidden behind some complicated network. What you want to do is take aim at one part of the group—a leader, a spokesman, a key member of the inner circle. Never aim at a vague, abstract enemy. It is hard to drum up the emotions to fight such a bloodless battle, which in any case leaves your enemy invisible. Personalize the fight, eyeball to eyeball.

Enemies bring many gifts. For one thing, they motivate you and focus your beliefs. Enemies also give you a standard by which to judge yourself, both personally and socially; it took Joe Frazier to make Muhammad Ali

opposition gives us inner satisfaction, distraction, relief ... Our opposition makes us feel that we are not completely victims of the circumstances.

GEORG SIMMEL, 1858–1918

a truly great fighter. A tough opponent will bring out the best in you. And the bigger the opponent, the greater your reward, even in defeat. It is better to lose to a worthy opponent than to squash some harmless foe. You will gain sympathy and respect, building support for your next fight.

Being attacked is a sign that you are important enough to be a target. You should relish the attention and the chance to prove yourself. Leaders have always found it useful to have an enemy at their gates in times of trouble, distracting the public from their difficulties. In using your enemies to rally your troops, polarize them as far as possible: they will fight the more fiercely when they feel a little hatred. So exaggerate the differences between you and the enemy—draw the lines clearly. Victory is your goal, not fairness and balance. Use the rhetoric of war to heighten the stakes and stimulate the spirit.

What you want in warfare is room to maneuver. Tight corners spell death. Having enemies gives you options. You can play them off against each other, make one a friend as a way of attacking the other. Without enemies you will not know how or where to maneuver, and you will lose a sense of your limits, of how far you can go.

Remember: there are always people out there who are more aggressive, more devious, more ruthless than you are, and it is inevitable that some of them will cross your path. You will have a tendency to want to conciliate and compromise with them. With some people you have to harden yourself, to recognize that there is no middle ground, no hope of conciliation. For your opponent your desire to compromise is a weapon to use against you.

Image:
The Earth. The
enemy is the ground
beneath your feet. It has a
gravity that holds you in place,
a force of resistance. Root yourself deep in this earth to gain
firmness and strength. Without
an enemy to walk upon, to
trample, you lose your bear-
ings and all sense of
proportion.

Authority: If you count on safety and do not think of danger, if you do not know enough to be wary when enemies arrive, this is called a sparrow nesting on a tent, a fish swimming in a cauldron—they won't last the day. —*Chuko Liang* (A.D. *181–234)*

2

DO NOT FIGHT THE LAST WAR THE GUERRILLA-WAR-OF-THE-MIND STRATEGY

What most often weighs you down and brings you misery is the past, in the form of unnecessary attachments, repetitions of tired formulas, and the memory of old victories and defeats. You must consciously wage war against the past and force yourself to react to the present moment. Be ruthless on yourself; do not repeat the same tired methods. Sometimes you must force yourself to strike out in new directions, even if they involve risk. What you may lose in comfort and security, you will gain in surprise, making it harder for your enemies to tell what you will do. Wage guerrilla war on your mind, allowing no static lines of defense, no exposed citadels—make everything fluid and mobile.

To know that one is in a certain condition, in a certain state, is already a process of liberation; but a man who is not aware of his condition, of his struggle, tries to be something other than he is, which brings about habit. So, then, let us keep in mind that we want to examine what is, to observe and be aware of exactly what is the actual, without giving it any slant, without giving it an interpretation. It needs an extraordinarily astute mind, an extraordinarily pliable heart, to be aware of and to follow what is; because what is is constantly moving, constantly undergoing a transformation, and if the mind is tethered to belief, to knowledge, it ceases to pursue, it ceases

KEYS TO WARFARE

In looking back on an unpleasant or disagreeable experience, the thought inevitably occurs to us: if only we had said or done *x* instead of *y*, if only we could do it over. Many a general has lost his head in the heat of battle and then, looking back, has thought of the one tactic, the one maneuver, that would have changed it all. The problem, though, is not that we think of the solution only when it is too late. The problem is that we imagine that knowledge is what was lacking. That is precisely the wrong approach. What makes us go astray in the first place is that we are unattuned to the present moment, insensitive to the circumstances. We are listening to our own thoughts, reacting to things that happened in the past, applying theories and ideas that we digested long ago but that have nothing to do with our predicament in the present.

Understand: the greatest generals, the most creative strategists, stand out not because they have more knowledge but because they are able, when necessary, to drop their preconceived notions and focus intensely on the present moment. That is how creativity is sparked and opportunities are seized. The better we can adapt our thoughts to changing circumstances, the more realistic our responses to them will be.

Reexamine all your cherished beliefs and principles. When Napoleon was asked what principles of war he followed, he replied that he followed none. His genius was his ability to respond to circumstances, to make the most of what he was given—he was the supreme opportunist. Your only principle, similarly, should be to have no principles.

When you are faced with a new situation, it is often best to imagine that you know nothing and that you need to start learning all over again. You will develop your own strategic muscles instead of depending on other people's theories and books.

Erase the memory of the last war. The last war you fought is a danger, even if you won it. It is fresh in your mind. If you were victorious, you will tend to repeat the strategies you just used, for success makes us lazy and complacent; if you lost, you may be skittish and indecisive. Do not think about the last war; you do not have the distance or the detachment. Instead do whatever you can to blot it from your mind.

Keep the mind moving. When we were children, our minds never stopped. We were open to new experiences and absorbed as much of them as possible.

All the greatest strategists were childlike in this respect. Sometimes, in fact, they even acted like children. The reason is simple: superior strategists see things as they are. They are highly sensitive to dangers and opportunities. Nothing stays the same in life, and keeping up with circumstances as they change requires a great deal of mental fluidity. Great strategists do not act according to preconceived ideas; they respond to the moment like children. Their minds are always moving, and they are always excited and curious. They quickly forget the past—the present is much too interesting.

to follow the swift movement of what is. What is is not static, surely—it is constantly moving, as you will see if you observe it very closely. To follow it, you need a very swift mind and a pliable heart—which are denied when the mind is static, fixed in a belief, in a prejudice, in an identification; and a mind and heart that are dry cannot follow easily, swiftly, that which is.

JIDDU
KRISHNAMURTI,
1895–1986

My policy is to have no policy.

ABRAHAM
LINCOLN,
1809–1865

Whenever you find your thoughts revolving around a particular subject or idea—an obsession, a resentment—force them past it. Distract yourself with something else. Like a child, find something new to be absorbed by, something worthy of concentrated attention. Do not waste time on things you cannot change or influence. Just keep moving.

Absorb the spirit of the times. Attune yourself to the spirit of the times. Developing antennae for the trends that have yet to crest takes work and study, as well as the flexibility to adapt to those trends. As you get older, it is best to periodically alter your style. By constantly adapting you will avoid the pitfalls of your previous wars. Just when people feel they know you, you will change.

Reverse course. Sometimes you have to shake yourself up, break free from the hold of the past. This can take the form of reversing your course, doing the opposite of what you would normally do in any given situation. In those situations the mind has to deal with a new reality, and it snaps to life.

Think of your mind as an army. Armies must adapt to the complexity and chaos of modern war by becoming more fluid and maneuverable. The ultimate extension of this evolution is guerrilla warfare, which exploits chaos by making disorder and unpredictability a strategy. The guerrilla army never stops to defend a particular place or town; it wins by always moving, staying one step ahead. By following no set pattern, it gives the enemy no target.

That is the model for your new way of

thinking. Apply no tactic rigidly. Attack problems from new angles, adapting to the landscape and to what you're given. By staying in constant motion you show your enemies no target to aim at.

Image: Water.
    Adapting its shape
       to wherever it
     moves in
          the stream,
          pushing
       rocks out of
         its way, smoothing
         boulders,
               it never stops,
                  is never the same.
                     The faster it moves
                       the clearer
                           it gets.

Authority: Some of our generals failed because they worked out everything by rule. They knew what Frederick did at one place, and Napoleon at another. They were always thinking about what Napoleon would do. . . . I don't underrate the value of military knowledge, but if men make war in slavish observance to rules, they will fail. . . . War is progressive.   *—Ulysses S. Grant (1822–85)*

3

AMIDST THE TURMOIL OF EVENTS, DO NOT LOSE YOUR PRESENCE OF MIND
THE COUNTERBALANCE STRATEGY

In the heat of battle, the mind tends to lose its balance. Too many things confront you at the same time—unexpected setbacks, doubts and criticisms from your own allies. There's a danger of responding emotionally, with fear, depression, or frustration. It is vital to keep your presence of mind, maintaining your mental powers whatever the circumstances. You must actively resist the emotional pull of the moment— staying decisive, confident, and aggressive no matter what hits you. Make the mind tougher by exposing it to adversity. Learn to detach yourself from the chaos of the battlefield. Let others lose their heads; your presence of mind will steer you clear of their influence and keep you on course.

KEYS TO WARFARE

We humans like to see ourselves as rational creatures. We imagine that what separates us from animals is the ability to think and reason. But that is only partly true: what distinguishes us from animals just as much is our capacity to laugh, to cry, to feel a range of emotions.

We maintain the illusion that we are rational through the routine of our daily affairs, which helps us to keep things calm and apparently controlled. But place any of us in an adverse situation and our rationality vanishes; we react to pressure by growing fearful, impatient, confused.

Understand: your mind is weaker than your emotions. But you become aware of this weakness only in moments of adversity—precisely the time when you need strength. What best equips you to cope with the heat of battle is neither more knowledge nor more intellect. What makes your mind stronger, and more able to control your emotions, is internal discipline and toughness.

No one can teach you this skill; you cannot learn it by reading about it. Like any discipline, it can come only through practice, experience, even a little suffering. Think of the following ideas as exercises, ways to toughen your mind, each a kind of counterbalance to emotion's overpowering pull.

Expose yourself to conflict. It is better to confront your fears, let them come to the surface, than to ignore them or tamp them down. Fear is the most destructive emotion for presence of mind, but it thrives on the unknown, which lets our imaginations run wild. By

The first quality of a General-in-Chief is to have a cool head which receives exact impressions of things, which never gets heated, which never allows itself to be dazzled, or intoxicated, by good or bad news. The successive simultaneous sensations which he receives in the course of a day must be classified, and must occupy the correct places they merit to fill, because common sense and reason are the results of the comparison of a number of sensations each equally well considered. There are certain men who, on account of their moral and physical constitution, paint mental pictures out of everything: however exalted be their reason, deliberately putting yourself in situations where you have to face fear, you familiarize yourself with it and your anxiety grows less acute. The sensation of overcoming a deep-rooted fear in turn gives you confidence and presence of mind. The more conflicts and difficult situations you put yourself through, the more battle-tested your mind will be.

Be self-reliant. There is nothing worse than feeling dependent on other people. Dependency makes you vulnerable to all kinds of emotions—betrayal, disappointment, frustration—that play havoc with your mental balance.

Being self-reliant is critical. To make yourself less dependent on others and so-called experts, you need to expand your repertoire of skills. And you need to feel more confident in your own judgment. Understand: we tend to overestimate other people's abilities and we tend to underestimate our own. You must compensate for this by trusting yourself more and others less.

It is important to remember, though, that being self-reliant does not mean burdening yourself with petty details. You must be able to distinguish between small matters that are best left to others and larger issues that require your attention and care.

Suffer fools gladly. You cannot be everywhere or fight everyone. Your time and energy are limited, and you must learn how to preserve them. Exhaustion and frustration can ruin your presence of mind. The world is full of fools—people who cannot wait to get results, who change with the wind, who can't

their will, their courage, and whatever good qualities they may possess, nature has not fitted them to command armies, nor to direct great operations of war.

NAPOLEON BONAPARTE, 1769–1821

see past their noses. When working alongside fools, do not fight them. Instead think of them the way you think of children, or pets, not important enough to affect your mental balance.

Crowd out feelings of panic by focusing on simple tasks. When circumstances scare us, our imagination tends to take over, filling our minds with endless anxieties. You need to gain control of your imagination, something easier said than done. Often the best way to calm down and give yourself such control is to force the mind to concentrate on something relatively simple—a calming ritual, a repetitive task that you are good at. You are creating the kind of composure you naturally have when your mind is absorbed in a problem. A focused mind has no room for anxiety or for the effects of an overactive imagination.

Unintimidate yourself. Intimidation will always threaten your presence of mind. And it is a hard feeling to combat.

The key to staying unintimidated is to convince yourself that the person you're facing is a mere mortal, no different from you. See the person, not the myth. Cutting the other person down to size will help you to keep your mental balance.

Develop your *Fingerspitzengefühl* (fingertip feel). Presence of mind depends not only on your mind's ability to come to your aid in difficult situations but also on the speed with which this happens. "Speed" here means responding to circumstances with rapidity and making lightning-quick decisions. This power is often read as a kind of intuition, what the Germans call "*Fingerspitzengefühl*" (fingertip feel).

There are things you can do to help you respond faster and bring out that intuitive feel that all animals possess. Deep knowledge of the terrain will let you process information faster than your enemy, a tremendous advantage. Getting a feel for the spirit of men and material, thinking your way into them instead of looking at them from outside, will help to put you in a different frame of mind, less conscious and forced, more unconscious and intuitive. Get your mind into the habit of making lightning-quick decisions, trusting your fingertip feel.

Finally, do not think of presence of mind as a quality useful only in periods of adversity, something to switch on and off as you need it. Cultivate it as an everyday condition. The better you get at the game of war, the more your warrior frame of mind will do for you in daily life. When a crisis does come, your mind will already be calm and prepared. Once presence of mind becomes a habit, it will never abandon you.

On a famous occasion during the civil war, Caesar tripped when disembarking from a ship on the shores of Africa and fell flat on his face. With his talent for improvisation, he spread out his arms and embraced the earth as a symbol of conquest. By quick thinking he turned a terrible omen of failure into one of victory.

CICERO: THE LIFE AND TIMES OF ROME'S GREATEST POLITICIAN, ANTHONY EVERITT, 2001

Image:
The Wind.
The rush of
unexpected events,
and the doubts and
criticisms of those around you,
are like a fierce wind at sea. It can
come from any point of the compass, and
there is no place to go to escape from it, no
way to predict when and in what direction it will
strike. To change direction with each gust of wind will
only throw you out to sea. Good pilots do not waste
time worrying about what they cannot control.
They concentrate on themselves, the skill
and steadiness of their hand, the
course they have plotted, and
their determination to
reach port, come
what may.

> **Authority:** A great part of courage is the courage of having done the thing before.
> —*Ralph Waldo Emerson (1803–82)*

4

CREATE A SENSE OF URGENCY AND DESPERATION THE DEATH-GROUND STRATEGY

You are your own worst enemy. You waste precious time dreaming of the future instead of engaging in the present. Since nothing seems urgent to you, you are only half involved in what you do. The only way to change is through action and outside pressure. Put yourself in situations where you have too much at stake to waste time or resources— if you cannot afford to lose, you won't. Cut your ties to the past; enter unknown territory where you must depend on your wits and energy to see you through. Place yourself on "death ground," where your back is against the wall and you have to fight like hell to get out alive.

KEYS TO WARFARE

Quite often we feel somewhat lost in our actions. We could do this or that—we have many options, but none of them seem quite necessary. Our freedom is a burden. Upon occasion all of us have felt a sense of urgency. Most often it is imposed from outside. Now everything changes; no more freedom. We have to do this, we have to fix that. The surprise is always how much more spirited and more alive this makes us feel; now everything we do seems necessary.

Leaders of armies have thought about this subject since armies existed: how can soldiers be motivated, be made more aggressive, more desperate? Some generals have relied on fiery oratory, and those particularly good at it have had some success. But over two thousand years ago, the Chinese strategist Sun-tzu came to believe that listening to speeches, no matter how rousing, was too passive an experience to have an enduring effect. Instead Sun-tzu talked of a "death ground"— a place where an army is backed up and has no escape route. Without a way to retreat, Sun-tzu argued, an army fights with double or triple the spirit it would have on open terrain, because death is viscerally present.

Death ground is a psychological phenomenon that goes well beyond the battlefield: it is any set of circumstances in which you feel enclosed and without options. You must act or suffer the consequences.

Understand: we are creatures who are intimately tied to our environment—we respond viscerally to our circumstances and to the people around us. If our situation is easy and relaxed, if people are friendly and warm, our natural tension unwinds. But put yourself in a high-stakes situation—a psychological death ground—and the dynamic changes. Your body responds to danger with a surge of energy; your mind focuses.

The trick is to use this effect deliberately from time to time, to practice it on yourself as a kind of wake-up call. The following five actions are designed to put you on a psychological death ground.

Stake everything on a single throw. Often we try too many things at one time, thinking that one of them will bring us success—but in these situations our minds are diffused, our efforts halfhearted. It is better to take on one daunting challenge, even one that others think foolish. Our future is at stake; we cannot afford to lose. So we don't.

Act before you are ready. We often wait too long to act, particularly when we face no outside pressure. It is sometimes better to act before you think you are ready—to force the issue. Not only will you take your opponents by surprise, you will also have to make the most of your resources. You have committed yourself and cannot turn back.

Enter new waters. You sometimes have to force yourself to leave stale relationships and comfortable situations behind, cutting your ties to the past. If you give yourself no way out, you will have to make your new endeavor work.

Make it "you against the world." A fighting spirit needs a little edge, some anger and

Lord Naoshige said, "The Way of the Samurai is in desperateness. Ten men or more cannot kill such a man. Common sense will not accomplish great things. Simply become insane and desperate."

HAGAKURE: THE BOOK OF THE SAMURAI, YAMAMOTO TSUNETOMO, 1659–1720

Death is nothing, but to live defeated is to die every day.

NAPOLEON BONAPARTE, 1769–1821

hatred to fuel it. So do not sit back and wait for people to get aggressive; irritate and infuriate them deliberately. Feeling cornered by a multitude of people who dislike you, you will fight like hell.

Keep yourself restless and unsatisfied. When we are tired, it is often because we are bored. When no real challenge faces us, a mental and physical lethargy sets in. Lack of energy comes from a lack of challenges, when we have taken on less than we are capable of. Take a risk and your body and mind will respond with a rush of energy. Make risk a constant practice; never let yourself settle down. Soon living on death ground will become a kind of addiction—you won't be able to do without it.

Image:
Fire. By itself it has
no force; it depends
on its environment.
Give it air, dry timber,
a wind to fan the
flames, and it gains a
terrifying momentum,
growing hotter, feeding off
itself, consuming everything
in its path. Never leave
such power to chance.

Authority: When you will survive if you fight quickly and perish if you do not, this is called [death] ground. . . . Put them in a spot where they have no place to go, and they will die before fleeing. If they are to die there, what can they not do? Warriors exert their full strength. When warriors are in great danger, then they have no fear. When there is nowhere to go, they are firm, when they are deeply involved, they stick to it. If they have no choice, they will fight. — *The Art of War, Sun-tzu (fourth century B.C.)*

When danger is greatest.—It is rare to break one's leg when in the course of life one is toiling upwards— it happens much more often when one starts to take things easy and to choose the easy paths.

FRIEDRICH NIETZSCHE, 1844–1900

PART
II

ORGANIZATIONAL (TEAM) WARFARE

You may have brilliant ideas, you may be able to invent unbeatable strategies—but if the group that you lead, and that you depend on to execute your plans, is unresponsive and uncreative, and if its members always put their personal agendas first, your ideas will mean nothing. You must learn the lesson of war: it is the structure of the army that will give your strategies force.

The primary goal in war is to build speed and mobility into the very structure of your army. That means having a single authority on top, avoiding the hesitancy and confusion of divided leadership. Finally, it means motivating soldiers, creating an overall esprit de corps that gives them irresistible momentum.

This military model is extremely adaptable to any group. It has one simple requirement: before formulating a strategy or taking action, understand the structure of your group. You can always change it and redesign it to fit your purposes. The following three chapters will help you focus on this critical issue and give you strategic options, as well as disastrous mistakes to avoid.

PART

II

ORGANIZATIONAL
(TEAM) WARFARE

5

AVOID THE SNARES OF GROUPTHINK THE COMMAND-AND-CONTROL STRATEGY

The problem in leading any group is that people inevitably have their own agendas. If you are too authoritarian, they will resent you and rebel in silent ways. If you are too easy-going, they will revert to their natural selfishness and you will lose control. You have to create a chain of command in which people do not feel constrained by your influence yet follow your lead. Put the right people in place—people who will enact the spirit of your ideas without being automatons. Make your commands clear and inspiring, focusing attention on the team, not the leader. Create a sense of participation, but do not fall into Groupthink—the irrationality of collective decision making. Make yourself look like a paragon of fairness, but never relinquish unity of command.

How very different is the cohesion between that of an army rallying around one flag carried into battle at the personal command of one general and that of an allied military force extending 50 or 100 leagues, or even on different sides of the theater! In the first case, cohesion is at its strongest and unity at its closest. In the second case, the unity is very remote, often consisting of no more than a shared political intention, and therefore only scanty and imperfect, while the cohesion of the parts is mostly weak and often no more than an illusion.

ON WAR, CARL VON CLAUSEWITZ, 1780–1831

Now more than ever, effective leadership requires a deft and subtle touch. The reason is simple: we have grown more distrustful of authority. At the same time, almost all of us imagine ourselves as authorities in our own right—officers, not foot soldiers. Feeling the need to assert themselves, people today put their own interests before the team. Group unity is fragile and can easily crack.

These trends affect leaders in ways they barely know. The tendency is to give more power to the group: wanting to seem democratic, leaders poll the whole staff for opinions, let the group make decisions, give subordinates input into the crafting of an overall strategy. Without realizing it, these leaders are letting the politics of the day seduce them into violating one of the most important rules of warfare and leadership: unity of command. Before it is too late, learn the lessons of war: divided leadership is a recipe for disaster, the cause of the greatest military defeats in history.

Divided leadership is dangerous because people in groups often think and act in ways that are illogical and ineffective—call it Groupthink. People in groups are political: they say and do things that they think will help their image within the group. They aim to please others, to promote themselves, rather than to see things dispassionately. Where an individual can be bold and creative, a group is often afraid of risk. The need to find a compromise among all the different egos kills creativity. The group has a mind of its own, and that mind is cautious, slow to decide, unimaginative, and sometimes downright irrational.

This is the game you must play: Do whatever you can to preserve unity of command. Keep the strings in your hands; the overarching strategic vision must come from you and you alone. At the same time, hide your tracks. Work behind the scenes; make the group feel involved in your decisions. Seek their advice, incorporating their good ideas, politely deflecting their bad ones.

A critical step in creating an efficient chain of command is assembling a skilled team that shares your goals and values. That team gives you many advantages: spirited, motivated people who can think on their own; an image as a delegator, a fair and democratic leader; and a saving in your own valuable energy, which you can redirect toward the larger picture.

In creating this team, you are looking for people who make up for your deficiencies, who have the skills you lack. Be careful in assembling this team that you are not seduced by expertise and intelligence. Character, the ability to work under you and with the rest of the team, and the capacity to accept responsibility and think independently are equally key. Rely on the team you have assembled, but do not be its prisoner or give it undue influence.

A key function of any chain of command is to supply information rapidly from the trenches, letting you adapt fast to circumstances. The shorter and more streamlined the chain of command, the better for the flow of information. Even so, information is often diluted as it passes up the chain.

What you need is what the military historian Martin van Creveld calls "a directed

Any army is like a horse, in that it reflects the temper and the spirit of its rider. If there is an uneasiness and an uncertainty, it transmits itself through the reins, and the horse feels uneasy and uncertain.

LONE STAR PREACHER, COLONEL JOHN W. THOMASON, JR., 1941

*"Do you think
every Greek here
can be a king?
It's no good
having a carload
of commanders.
We need
One commander,
one king, the one
to whom Zeus,
Son of Cronus
the crooked, has
given the staff
And the right to
make decisions
for his people."
And so Odysseus
mastered the
army. The
men all
Streamed back
from their ships
and huts and
assembled
With a roar.*

THE ILIAD,
HOMER, CIRCA
NINTH CENTURY
B.C.

telescope": people in various parts of the chain, and elsewhere, to give you instant information from the battlefield. These people—an informal network of friends, allies, and spies—let you bypass the slow-moving chain.

The single greatest risk to your chain of command comes from the political animals in the group. People like this are inescapable; they spring up like weeds in any organization. Not only are they out for themselves, but they build factions to further their own agendas and fracture the cohesion you have built. Interpreting your commands for their own purposes, finding loopholes in any ambiguity, they create invisible breaks in the chain.

Try to weed them out before they arrive. In hiring your team, look at the candidates' histories: Are they restless? Do they often move from place to place? That is a sign of the kind of ambition that will keep them from fitting in. When people seem to share your ideas exactly, be wary: they are probably mirroring them to charm you.

Another solution is to isolate the political moles—to give them no room to maneuver within the organization. Once you identify the moles in the group, you must act fast to stop them from building a power base from which to destroy your authority.

Finally, pay attention to the orders themselves—their form as well as their substance. Vague orders are worthless. As they pass from person to person, they are hopelessly altered, and your staff comes to see them as symbolizing uncertainty and indecision. On the other hand, if your commands are too specific and too narrow, you will encourage people to behave like automatons and stop thinking for themselves.

Clear, concise, inspiring orders make officers feel in control and fill troops with fighting spirit.

Image: The Reins. A horse with no bridle is useless, but equally bad is the horse whose reins you pull at every turn, in a vain effort at control. Control comes from almost letting go, holding the reins so lightly that the horse feels no tug but senses the slightest change in tension and responds as you desire. Not everyone can master such an art.

Authority: Better one bad general than two good ones. *—Napoleon Bonaparte (1769–1821)*

6

SEGMENT YOUR FORCES
THE CONTROLLED-CHAOS
STRATEGY

The critical elements in war are speed and adaptability—the ability to move and make decisions faster than the enemy. But speed and adaptability are hard to achieve today. We have more information than ever before at our fingertips, making interpretation and decision making more difficult. We have more people to manage, those people are more widely spread, and we face more uncertainty. Learn from Napoleon, warfare's greatest master: speed and adaptability come from flexible organization. Break your forces into independent groups that can operate and make decisions on their own. Make your forces elusive and unstoppable by infusing them with the spirit of the campaign, giving them a mission to accomplish, and then letting them run.

KEYS TO WARFARE

The essence of strategy is not to carry out a brilliant plan that proceeds in steps; it is to put yourself in situations where you have more options than the enemy does. A rigid, centralized organization locks you into linear strategies; a fluid, segmented army gives you options. Structure *is* strategy—perhaps the most important strategic choice you will make. Should you inherit a group, analyze its structure and alter it to suit your purposes. Pour your creative energy into its organization, making fluidity your goal.

The German general staff, which was in place from 1808 to the end of World War II, during which period the Germans consistently outfought other armies in the field, should serve as the organizational model for any group that aims at mobility and strategic depth. First, the staff's structure was fluid, allowing its leaders to adapt it to their own needs. Second, it examined itself constantly and modified itself according to what it had learned. Third, it replicated its structure through the rest of the army: its officers trained the officers below them, and so on down the line. The smallest team was inculcated with the overall philosophy of the group. Finally, rather than issuing rigid orders, the staff embraced the mission command: a statement of overall mission, a directive to be followed in its spirit, not its letter. By making officers and soldiers feel more creatively engaged, this tactic improved their performance and sped up the decision-making process. Mobility was written into the system.

The key is an overall group philosophy.

This can be built around the cause you are fighting for or a belief in the evil of the enemy you face. You must bring the group together around this belief. Find exercises to increase your troops' knowledge of and trust in each other. This will develop implicit communication skills between them and their intuitive sense of what to do next. Do not confuse a chummy, clublike atmosphere with team spirit and cohesion. Coddling your soldiers and acting as if everyone were equal will ruin discipline and promote the creation of factions.

Finally, you need to structure your group according to your soldiers' strengths and weaknesses, to their social circumstances. Do not struggle with your soldiers' idiosyncrasies, but rather turn them into a virtue, a way to increase your potential force.

Patton's philosophy of command was: "Never tell people how to do things. Tell them what to do and they will surprise you with their ingenuity."

PATTON: A GENIUS FOR WAR, CARLO D'ESTE, 1995

Image:
The Spider's Web.
Most animals attack along a
straight line; the spider weaves
a web, adapted to its location and
spun in a pattern, whether simple or
complex. Once the web is woven, the
work is done. The spider has no
need to hunt; it simply waits for
the next fool to fall into the
web's barely visible
strands.

Authority: Thus the army . . . moves for advantage, and changes through segmenting and reuniting. Thus its speed is like the wind, its slowness like the forest; its invasion and plundering like a fire. . . . It is as difficult to know as the darkness; in movement it is like thunder.

— *The Art of War, Sun-tzu, (fourth century B.C.)*

7

TRANSFORM YOUR WAR
INTO A CRUSADE
MORALE STRATEGIES

The secret to motivating people and maintaining their morale is to get them to think less about themselves and more about the group. Involve them in a cause, a crusade against a hated enemy. Make them see their survival as tied to the success of the army as a whole. In a group in which people have truly bonded, moods and emotions are so contagious that it becomes easy to infect your troops with enthusiasm. Lead from the front: let your soldiers see you in the trenches, making sacrifices for the cause. That will fill them with the desire to emulate and please you. Make both rewards and punishments rare but meaningful. Remember: a motivated army can work wonders, making up for any lack of material resources.

You can do nothing with an army that is an amalgam of a hundred people here, a hundred people there, and so on. What can be achieved with four thousand men, united and standing shoulder to shoulder, you cannot do with forty or even four hundred thousand men who are divided and pulled this way and that by internal conflicts....

RULES OF WAR AND BRAVERY, MUBARAKSHAH, PERSIA, THIRTEENTH CENTURY

We humans are selfish by nature. Our first thoughts in any situation revolve around our own interests: How will this affect *me*? How will it help *me*? At the same time, by necessity, we try to disguise our selfishness, making our motives look altruistic or disinterested. Our inveterate selfishness and our ability to disguise it are problems for you as a leader. You may think that the people working for you are genuinely enthusiastic and concerned—that is what they say, that is what their actions suggest. Then slowly you see signs that this person or that is using his or her position in the group to advance purely personal interests. One day you wake up to find yourself leading an army of selfish, conniving individuals.

That is when you start thinking about morale—about finding a way to motivate your troops and forge them into a group. Perhaps you try artfully to praise people, to offer them the possibility of reward—only to find you have spoiled them, strengthening their selfishness. Perhaps you try punishments and discipline—only to make them resentful and defensive. Perhaps you try to fire them up with speeches and group activities—but people are cynical nowadays; they will see right through you.

The problem is not what you are doing but the fact that it comes late. You have begun to think about morale only after it has become an issue, not before. That is your mistake. Learn from history's great motivators and military leaders: the way to get soldiers to work together and maintain morale is to make them feel part of a group that is fighting for a worthy cause. That distracts them from their own interests and satisfies their human need to feel part of something bigger than they are. The more they think of the group, the less they think of themselves. They soon begin to link their own success to the group's; their own interests and the larger interests coincide. In this kind of army, people know that selfish behavior will disgrace them in the eyes of their companions. They become attuned to a kind of group conscience.

Morale is contagious: put people in a cohesive, animated group and they naturally catch that spirit. If they rebel or revert to selfish behavior, they are easily isolated. You must establish this dynamic the minute you become the group's leader; it can only come from the top—that is, from you.

The ability to create the right group dynamic, to maintain the collective spirit, is known in military language as "man management."

To create the best group dynamic and prevent destructive morale problems, follow these eight crucial steps culled from the writings and experiences of the masters of the art.

Step 1: Unite your troops around a cause. Make them fight for an idea. Now more than ever, people have a hunger to believe in something. They feel an emptiness, which, left alone, they might try to fill with drugs or spiritual fads, but you can take advantage of it by channeling it into a cause you can convince them is worth fighting for. Bring people together around a cause and you create a motivated force.

What stronger breastplate than a heart untainted! Thrice is he arm'd that hath his quarrel just, And he but naked, though lock'd up in steel, Whose conscience with injustice is corrupted.

KING HENRY V,
WILLIAM
SHAKESPEARE,
1564–1616

The cause can be anything you wish, but you should represent it as progressive: it fits the times, it is on the side of the future, so it is destined to succeed. If necessary, you can give it a veneer of spirituality. It is best to have some kind of enemy to hate—an enemy can help a group to define itself in opposition. Ignore this step and you are left with an army of mercenaries. You will deserve the fate that usually awaits such armies.

Step 2: Keep their bellies full. People cannot stay motivated if their material needs go unmet. If they feel exploited in any way, their natural selfishness will come to the surface and they will begin to peel off from the group. Use a cause—something abstract or spiritual—to bring them together, but meet their material needs. You do not have to spoil them by overpaying them; a paternalistic feeling that they are being taken care of, that you are thinking of their comfort, is more important. Attending to their physical needs will make it easier to ask more of them when the time comes.

Step 3: Lead from the front. The enthusiasm with which people join a cause inevitably wanes. One thing that speeds up its loss, and that produces discontent, is the feeling that the leaders do not practice what they preach. Right from the beginning, your troops must see you leading from the front, sharing their dangers and sacrifices—taking the cause as seriously as they do. Instead of trying to push them from behind, make them run to keep up with you.

There are always moments when the commander's place is not back with his staff but up with the troops. It is sheer nonsense to say that maintenance of the men's morale is the job of the battalion commander alone. The higher the rank, the greater the effect of the example. The men tend to feel no kind of contact with a commander who, they know, is sitting somewhere in headquarters. What they want is what might be termed a physical contact with him. In moments of panic, fatigue, or disorganization, or when something out of the ordinary has to be demanded from them, the personal example of the

Step 4: Concentrate their *ch'i.* There is a Chinese belief in an energy called ch'i, which dwells in all living things. All groups have their own level of ch'i, physical and psychological. A leader must understand this energy and know how to manipulate it.

Idleness has a terrible effect on ch'i. When soldiers are not working, their spirits lower. Doubts creep in, and selfish interests take over. Similarly, being on the defensive, always waiting and reacting to what the enemy dishes out, will also lower ch'i. So keep your soldiers busy, acting for a purpose, moving in a direction. Do not make them wait for the next attack; propelling them forward will excite them and make them hungry for battle. Aggressive action concentrates ch'i, and concentrated ch'i is full of latent force.

Step 5: Play to their emotions. The best way to motivate people is not through reason but through emotion. Humans, however, are naturally defensive, and if you begin with an appeal to their emotions—some histrionic harangue—they will see you as manipulative and will recoil. An emotional appeal needs a setup: lower their defenses, and make them bond as a group, by putting on a show, entertaining them, telling a story. Now they have less control over their emotions and you can approach them more directly, moving them easily from laughter to anger or hatred. Masters of man management have a sense of drama: they know when and how to hit their soldiers in the gut.

Step 6: Mix harshness and kindness. The key to man management is a balance of

commander works wonders, especially if he has had the wit to create some sort of legend around himself.

FIELD MARSHAL ERWIN ROMMEL, 1891–1944

punishment and reward. Too many rewards will spoil your soldiers and make them take you for granted; too much punishment will destroy their morale. You need to hit the right balance. Make your kindness rare and even an occasional warm comment or generous act will be powerfully meaningful. Anger and punishment should be equally rare; instead your harshness should take the form of setting very high standards that few can reach. Make your soldiers compete to please you. Make them struggle to see less harshness and more kindness.

Step 7: Build the group myth. The armies with the highest morale are armies that have been tested in battle. Soldiers who have fought alongside one another through many campaigns forge a kind of group myth based on their past victories. Living up to the tradition and reputation of the group becomes a matter of pride; anyone who lets it down feels ashamed. To generate this myth, you must lead your troops into as many campaigns as you can. It is wise to start out with easy battles that they can win, building up their confidence. Success alone will help bring the group together. Create symbols and slogans that fit the myth. Your soldiers will want to belong.

Step 8: Be ruthless with grumblers. Allow grumblers and the chronically disaffected any leeway at all and they will spread disquiet and even panic throughout the group. As fast as you can, you must isolate them and get rid of them. All groups contain a core of people who are more motivated and disciplined than the rest—your best soldiers. Recognize them, cultivate their goodwill, and set them up as examples. These people will serve as natural ballasts against those who are disaffected and panicky.

Image:
The Ocean's Tide. It
ebbs and flows so power-
fully that no one in its path
can escape its pull or move
against it. Like the moon, you
are the force that sets the
tide, which carries everything along in its
wake.

Authority: The Way means inducing the people to have the same aim as the leadership, so that they will share death and share life, without fear of danger. *—Sun-tzu (fourth century B.C.)*

PART

III

DEFENSIVE WARFARE

To fight in a defensive manner is not a sign of weakness; it is the height of strategic wisdom, a powerful style of waging war. Its requirements are simple: First, you must make the most of your resources, fighting with perfect economy and engaging only in battles that are necessary. Second, you must know how and when to retreat, luring an aggressive enemy into an imprudent attack. Then, waiting patiently for his moment of exhaustion, launch a vicious counterattack.

To fight this way, you must master the arts of deception. By seeming weaker than you are, you can draw the enemy into an ill-advised attack; by seeming stronger than you are, you can deter the enemy from attacking you. In defensive warfare you are essentially leveraging your weaknesses and limitations into power and victory.

The following four chapters will instruct you in the basic arts of defensive warfare: economy of means, counterattack, intimidation and deterrence, and how to retreat skillfully and lie low when under aggressive attack.

8

PICK YOUR BATTLES CAREFULLY THE PERFECT-ECONOMY STRATEGY

We all have limitations—our energies and skills will take us only so far. Danger comes from trying to surpass our limits. Seduced by some glittering prize into overextending ourselves, we end up exhausted and vulnerable. You must know your limits and pick your battles carefully. Consider the hidden costs of a war: time lost, political goodwill squandered, an embittered enemy bent on revenge. Sometimes it is better to wait, to undermine your enemies covertly rather than hitting them straight on. If battle cannot be avoided, get them to fight on your terms. Aim at their weaknesses; make the war expensive for them and cheap for you. Fighting with perfect economy, you can outlast even the most powerful foe.

KEYS TO WARFARE

He whom the ancients called an expert in battle gained victory where victory was easily gained. Thus the battle of the expert is never an exceptional victory, nor does it win him reputation for wisdom or credit for courage. His victories in battle are unerring. Unerring means that he acts where victory is certain, and conquers an enemy that has already lost.

THE ART OF WAR, SUN-TZU, FOURTH CENTURY B.C.

Abundance makes us soft and decadent, bored with what we have and in need of constant shocks to remind us that we are alive. In life you must be a warrior, and war requires realism. While others may find beauty in endless dreams, warriors find it in reality, in awareness of limits, in making the most of what they have. They look for the perfect economy of motion and gesture—the way to give their blows the greatest force with the least expenditure of effort. Their awareness that their days are numbered—that they could die at any time—grounds them in reality.

Armies that seem to have the edge in money, resources, and firepower tend to be predictable. Relying on their equipment instead of on knowledge and strategy, they grow mentally lazy. When problems arise, their solution is to amass more of what they already have. But it's not what you have that brings you victory, it's how you use it. When you have less, you are naturally more inventive. Creativity gives you an edge over enemies dependent on technology; you will learn more, be more adaptable, and you will outsmart them. Unable to waste your limited resources, you will use them well. Time will be your ally.

If you have less than your enemy, do not despair. You can always turn the situation around by practicing perfect economy. If you and your enemy are equals, getting hold of more weaponry matters less than making better use of what you have. If you have more than your enemy, fighting economically is as important as ever.

War is a balance of ends and means: a general might have the best plan to achieve a certain end, but unless he has the means to accomplish it, his plan is worthless. Wise generals through the ages, then, have learned to begin by examining the means they have at hand and then to develop their strategy out of those tools.

The next time you launch a campaign, try an experiment: do not think about either your solid goals or your wishful dreams, and do not plan out your strategy on paper. Instead think deeply about what you have— the tools and materials you will be working with. Ground yourself not in dreams and plans but in reality: think of your own skills, any political advantage you might have, the morale of your troops, how creatively you can use the means at your disposal. Then, out of that process, let your plans and goals blossom. Not only will your strategies be more realistic, they will be more inventive and forceful. Dreaming first of what you want and then trying to find the means to reach it is a recipe for exhaustion, waste, and defeat.

Do not mistake cheapness for perfect economy—armies have failed by spending too little as often as by spending too much. Perfect economy does not mean hoarding your resources. That is not economy but stinginess—deadly in war. Perfect economy means finding a golden mean, a level at which your blows count but do not wear you out. Over-economizing will wear you out more, for the war will drag on, its costs growing, without your ever being able to deliver a knockout punch.

Several tactics lend themselves to

Achilles now routed the Trojans and pursued them towards the city, but his course, too, was run. Poseidon and Apollo, pledged to avenge the deaths of Cycnus and Troilus, and to punish certain insolent boasts that Achilles had uttered over Hector's corpse, took counsel together. Veiled with cloud and standing by the Scaean gate, Apollo sought out Paris in the thick of battle, turned his bow and guided the fatal shaft. It struck the one vulnerable part of Achilles's body, the right heel, and he died in agony.

THE GREEK MYTHS, VOL. 2, ROBERT GRAVES, 1955

economy in fighting. First is the use of deception, which costs relatively little but can yield powerful results. Deception can be a great equalizer for the weaker side. Its arts include the gathering of intelligence, the spreading of misinformation, and the use of propaganda to make the war more unpopular within the enemy camp.

Second, look for opponents you can beat. Avoid enemies who have nothing to lose—they will work to bring you down whatever it costs. Easy victories enhance morale, develop your reputation, give you momentum, and, most important, do not cost you much.

There will be times when your calculations misfire; what had seemed to be an easy campaign turns out hard. Not everything can be foreseen. Not only is it important to pick your battles carefully, then, but you must also know when to accept your losses and quit. Do not soldier on out of frustration or pride. Too much is at stake.

Fighting economically will build momentum. Think of it as finding your level—a perfect balance between what you are capable of and the task at hand. Knowing your limits will expand your limits; getting the most out of what you have will let you have more.

Image: The Swimmer. The water offers resistance; you can move only so fast. Some swimmers pound at the water, trying to use force to generate speed—but they only make waves, creating resistance in their path. Others are too delicate, kicking so lightly they barely move. Consummate swimmers hit the surface with perfect economy, keeping the water in front of them smooth and level. They move as fast as the water will let them and cover great distances at a steady pace.

Authority: The value of a thing sometimes lies not in what one attains with it but in what one pays for it—what it costs us.
—*Friedrich Nietzsche (1844–1900)*

9

TURN THE TABLES
THE COUNTERATTACK
STRATEGY

Moving first—initiating the attack—will often put you at a disadvantage: you are exposing your strategy and limiting your options. Instead discover the power of holding back and letting the other side move first, giving you the flexibility to counterattack from any angle. If your opponents are aggressive, bait them into a rash attack that will leave them in a weak position. Learn to use their impatience, their eagerness to get at you, as a way to throw them off balance and bring them down. In difficult moments do not despair or retreat: any situation can be turned around. If you learn how to hold back, waiting for the right moment to launch an unexpected counterattack, weakness can become strength.

A rapid,
powerful
transition to
the attack— the
glinting sword of
vengeance—is
the most brilliant
moment of
the defense.

CARL VON
CLAUSEWITZ,
1780–1831

KEYS TO WARFARE

Thousands of years ago, at the dawn of military history, various strategists in different cultures noticed a peculiar phenomenon: in battle, the side that was on the defensive often won in the end. There seemed to be several reasons for this. First, once the aggressor went on the attack, he had no more surprises in store—the defender could clearly see his strategy and take protective action. Second, if the defender could somehow turn back this initial attack, the aggressor would be left in a weak position; his army was disorganized and exhausted. (It requires more energy to take land than to hold it.) If the defenders could take advantage of this weakness to deliver a counterblow, they could often force the aggressor to retreat.

Based on these observations, the art of the counterattack was developed. Its basic tenets were to let the enemy make the first move, actively baiting him into an aggressive attack that would expend his energy and unbalance his lines, then taking advantage of his weakness and disorganization.

The counterattack is, in fact, the origin of modern strategy. The first real example of an indirect approach to war, it represents a major breakthrough in thinking: instead of being brutal and direct, the counterattack is subtle and deceptive, using the enemy's energy and aggression to bring about his downfall. Although it is one of the oldest and most basic strategies in warfare, it remains in many ways the most effective and has proven highly adaptable to modern conditions.

The counterattack principle is infinitely applicable to any competitive environment or form of conflict, since it is based on certain truths of human nature. We are inherently impatient creatures. We find it hard to wait; we want our desires to be satisfied as quickly as possible. This is a tremendous weakness, for it means that in any given situation we often commit ourselves without enough thought. In charging ahead we limit our options and get ourselves into trouble. Patience, on the other hand, particularly in war, pays unlimited dividends: it allows us to sniff out opportunities, to time a counterblow that will catch the enemy by surprise. A person who can lie back and wait for the right moment to take action will almost always have an advantage over those who give in to their natural impatience.

Once you learn patience, your options suddenly expand. Instead of wearing yourself out in little wars, you can save your energy for the right moment, take advantage of other people's mistakes, and think clearly in difficult situations. You will see opportunities for counterattack where others see only surrender or retreat.

The key to the successful counterattack is staying calm while your opponent gets frustrated and irritable. In sixteenth-century Japan, there emerged a novel way of fighting called Shinkage: the swordsman would begin the fight by mirroring his opponent's every move. Mirroring people—giving back to them just what they give you—is a powerful method of counterattack. In daily life, mirroring and passivity can charm people, flattering them into lowering their defenses and opening themselves to attack. It can also irritate and discomfit them.

When the enemy finds itself in a predicament and wants to engage us in a decisive battle, wait; when it is advantageous for the enemy but not for us to fight, wait; when it is expedient to remain still and whoever moves first will fall into danger, wait; when two enemies are engaged in a fight that will result in defeat or injury, wait; when the enemy forces, though numerous, suffer from mistrust and tend to plot against one another, wait; when the enemy commander, though wise, is handicapped by some of his cohorts, wait.

THE WILES OF WAR: 36 MILITARY STRATEGIES FROM ANCIENT CHINA, TRANSLATED BY SUN HAICHEN, 1991

The counterattack is a particularly effective strategy against what might be called "the barbarian"—the man or woman who is especially aggressive by nature. Do not be intimidated by these types; they are in fact weak and are easily swayed and deceived. The trick is to goad them by playing weak or stupid while dangling in front of them the prospect of easy gains.

Look for the emotion that your enemies are least able to manage, then bring it to the surface. With a little work on your part, they will lay themselves open to your counterattack.

Whenever you find yourself on the defensive and in trouble, the greatest danger is the impulse to overreact. You will often exaggerate your enemy's strength, seeing yourself as weaker than is actually the case. A key principle of counterattack is never to see a situation as hopeless. No matter how strong your enemies seem, they have vulnerabilities you can prey upon and use to develop a counterattack. Your own weakness can become a strength if you play it right.

An enemy seems powerful because he has a particular strength or advantage. Maybe it's money and resources; maybe it's the size of his army or of his territory; maybe, more subtly, it's his moral standing and reputation. Whatever his strength might be, it is actually a potential weakness, simply because he relies on it: neutralize it and he is vulnerable.

As you neutralize your enemy's strengths, you must similarly reverse your own weaknesses. If your forces are small, for example, they are also mobile; use that mobility to

The notion of "catching" (utsuraseru) applies to many things: yawning and sleepiness, for example. Time can also be "catching." In a large-scale battle, when the enemy is restless and trying to bring a quick conclusion to the battle, pay no attention. Instead, try to pretend that you are calm and quiet with no urgent need to end the battle. The enemy will then be affected by your calm and easy attitude and become less alert. When this "catching" occurs, quickly execute a strong attack to defeat the enemy.... There is also a concept called "making one drunk," which is similar to the notion of "catching." You can make your opponent feel bored, carefree, counterattack. Perhaps your reputation is lower than your opponent's; that just means you have less to lose. Sling mud—some of it will stick, and gradually your enemy will sink to your level. Always find ways to turn your weakness to advantage.

or feeble spirited. You should study these matters well.

THE BOOK OF FIVE RINGS, MIYAMOTO MUSASHI, 1584–1645

Image: The Bull. It is large, its stare is intimidating, and its horns can pierce your flesh. Attacking it and trying to escape it are equally fatal. Instead stand your ground and let the bull charge your cape, giving it nothing to hit, making its horns useless. Get it angry and irritated—the harder and more furiously it charges, the faster it wears itself down. A point will come when you can turn the game around and go to work, carving up the once fearsome beast.

Authority: The whole art of war consists in a well-reasoned and extremely circumspect defensive, followed by a rapid and audacious attack. —*Napoleon Bonaparte (1769–1821)*

10

CREATE A THREATENING PRESENCE DETERRENCE STRATEGIES

The best way to fight off aggressors is to keep them from attacking you in the first place. To accomplish this you must create the impression of being more powerful than you are. Build up a reputation: you're a little crazy; fighting you is not worth it; you take your enemies with you when you lose. Create this reputation and make it credible with a few impressive— impressively violent—acts. Uncertainty is sometimes better than overt threat: if your opponents are never sure what messing with you will cost, they will not want to find out. Play on people's natural fears and anxieties to make them think twice.

If your organization is small in numbers, then do what Gideon did: conceal the members in the dark but raise a din and clamor that will make the listener believe that your organization numbers many more than it does. . . . Always remember the first rule of power tactics: Power is not only what you have but what the enemy thinks you have.

RULES FOR RADICALS, SAUL D. ALINSKY, 1972

Inevitably in life you will find yourself facing people who are more aggressive than you are—crafty, ruthless people who are determined to get what they want. Fighting them head-on is generally foolish; fighting is what they are good at, and they are unscrupulous to boot. You will probably lose. Trying to fend them off by giving them part of what they are after, or otherwise pleasing or appeasing them, is a recipe for disaster: you are only showing your weakness, inviting more threats and attacks. But giving in completely, surrendering without a fight, hands them the easy victory they crave and makes you resentful and bitter. It can also become a bad habit, the path of least resistance in dealing with difficult situations.

Instead of trying to avoid conflict or whining about the injustice of it all, consider an option developed over the centuries by military leaders and strategists to deal with violent and acquisitive neighbors: reverse intimidation. This art of deterrence rests on three basic facts about war and human nature: First, people are more likely to attack you if they see you as weak or vulnerable. Second, they cannot know for sure that you're weak; they depend on the signs you give out, through your behavior both present and past. Third, they are after easy victories, quick and bloodless. That is why they prey on the vulnerable and weak.

Deterrence is simply a matter of turning this dynamic around, altering any perception of yourself as weak and naïve and sending the message that battle with you will not be as easy as they had thought. This is generally done by taking some visible action that will confuse aggressors and make them think they have misread you: you may indeed be vulnerable, but they are not sure. You're disguising your weakness and distracting them.

This form of defensive warfare is infinitely applicable to the battles of daily life. Appeasing people can be as debilitating as fighting them; deterring them, scaring them out of attacking you or getting in your way, will save you valuable energy and resources. To deter aggressors you must become adept at deception, manipulating appearances and their perceptions of you—valuable skills that can be applied to all aspects of daily warfare. And finally, by practicing the art as needed, you will build for yourself a reputation as someone tough, someone worthy of respect and a little fear.

The following are five basic methods of deterrence and reverse intimidation. You can use them all in offensive warfare, but they are particularly effective in defense, for moments when you find yourself vulnerable and under attack. They are culled from the experiences and writings of the greatest masters of the art.

Surprise with a bold maneuver. The best way to hide your weakness and to bluff your enemies into giving up their attack is to take some unexpected, bold, risky action. Perhaps they had thought you were vulnerable, and now you are acting as someone who is fearless and confident. This will have two positive effects: First, they will tend to think your move is backed up by something real—they will not imagine you could be foolish enough

Brinkmanship is . . . the deliberate creation of a recognizable risk, a risk that one does not completely control. It is the tactic of deliberately letting the situation get somewhat out of hand, just because its being out of hand may be intolerable to the other party and force his accommodation. It means harassing and intimidating an adversary by exposing him to a shared risk, or deterring him by showing that if he makes a contrary move he may disturb us so that we slip over the brink whether we want to or not, carrying him with us.

THINKING STRATEGICALLY.
AVINASH K.
DIXIT AND BARRY
J. NALEBUFF, 1991

A certain
person said the
following.
There are
two kinds of
dispositions,
inward and
outward, and a
person who is
lacking in one
or the other is
worthless. It is,
for example,
like the blade of
a sword, which
one should
sharpen well
and then put
in its scabbard,
periodically
taking it out
and knitting
one's eyebrows
as in an attack,
wiping off the
blade, and then
placing it in its
scabbard again.
If a person has
his sword out
all the time, he
is habitually
swinging a
naked blade;
people will not
approach him
and he will have
no allies. If a
sword is always
sheathed, it will
become rusty, the
blade will dull,
and people will

to do something audacious just for effect. Second, they will start to see strengths and threats in you that they had not imagined.

Reverse the threat. If your enemies see you as someone to be pushed around, turn the tables with a sudden move, however small, designed to scare them. Threaten something they value. Hit them where you sense they may be vulnerable, and make it hurt. If that infuriates them and makes them attack you, back off a moment and then hit them again when they're not expecting it. Show them you are not afraid of them and that you are capable of a ruthlessness they had not seen in you.

Seem unpredictable and irrational. In this instance you do something suggesting a slightly suicidal streak, as if you felt you had nothing to lose. You show that you are ready to take your enemies down with you, destroying their reputations in the process. (This is particularly effective with people who have a lot to lose themselves—powerful people with sterling reputations.) To defeat you will be costly and perhaps self-destructive. This will make fighting you very unattractive. Crazy opponents are terrifying—no one likes fighting people who are unpredictable and have nothing to lose.

Play on people's natural paranoia. Instead of threatening your opponents openly, you take action that is indirect and designed to make them think. This might mean using a go-between to send them a message—to tell some disturbing story about what you are capable of. Or maybe you "inadvertently" let them spy on you, only to hear something that should give them cause for concern. Making your enemies think they have found out you are plotting a countermove is more effective than telling them so yourself. The more veiled menace and uncertainty you generate, the more their imaginations will run away with them and the more dangerous an attack on you will seem.

Establish a frightening reputation. This reputation can be for any number of things: being difficult, stubborn, violent, ruthlessly efficient. Build up that image over the years and people will back off from you, treating you with respect and a little fear. You must build your reputation carefully, allowing no inconsistencies. Any holes in this kind of image will make it worthless.

think as much of its owner.

HAGAKURE: THE BOOK OF THE SAMURAI, YAMAMOTO TSUNETOMO, 1659–1720

Image:
The Porcupine. It seems rather stupid and slow, easy prey, but when it is threatened or attacked, its quills stand erect. If touched, they come out easily in your flesh, and trying to extract them makes their hooked ends go deeper and deeper, causing still more damage. Those who have fought with a porcupine learn never to repeat the experience. Even without fighting it, most people know to avoid it and leave it in peace.

Authority: When opponents are unwilling to fight with you, it is because they think it is contrary to their interests, or because you have misled them into thinking so.
— *Sun-tzu (fourth century B.C.)*

11

TRADE SPACE FOR TIME
THE NONENGAGEMENT
STRATEGY

Retreat in the face of a strong enemy is a sign not of weakness but of strength. By resisting the temptation to respond to an aggressor, you buy yourself valuable time—time to recover, to think, to gain perspective. Let your enemies advance; time is more important than space. By refusing to fight, you infuriate them and feed their arrogance. They will soon overextend themselves and start making mistakes. Time will reveal them as rash and you as wise. Sometimes you can accomplish most by doing nothing.

KEYS TO WARFARE

The problem we all face in strategy, and in life, is that each of us is unique and has a unique personality. Our circumstances are also unique; no situation ever really repeats itself. But most often we are barely aware of what makes us different—in other words, of who we really are.

Your task as a strategist is simple: to see the differences between yourself and other people, to understand yourself, your side, and the enemy as well as you can, to get more perspective on events, to know things for what they are. In the hubbub of daily life, this is not easy—in fact, the power to do it can come only from knowing when and how to retreat. If you are always advancing, always attacking, always responding to people emotionally, you have no time to gain perspective.

When you fight someone more powerful than you are, you lose more than your possessions and position; you lose your ability to think straight, to keep yourself separate and distinct. You become infected with the emotions and violence of the aggressor in ways you cannot imagine. Better to flee and use the time your flight buys to turn inward. Let the enemy take land and advance; you will recover and turn the tables when the time comes. The decision to retreat shows not weakness but strength. It is the height of strategic wisdom.

Most people respond to aggression by in some way getting involved with it. It is almost impossible to hold back. By disengaging completely and retreating, you show great power and restraint. Your enemies are desperate for you to react; retreat infuriates and provokes them into further attack. So keep retreating, exchanging space for time. Stay calm and balanced. Time is on your side, for you are not wasting any of it in useless battles. Time is just as important as space in strategic thought, and knowing how to use time will make you a superior strategist, giving an added dimension to your attacks and defense. To waste your time in battles not of your choosing is more than just a mistake, it is stupidity of the highest order. Time lost can never be regained.

> **Image:** The Desert Sands. In the
> desert there is nothing to feed
> on and nothing to use for war:
> just sand and empty space.
> Retreat to the desert occasion-
> ally, to think and see
> with clarity.
> Time
> moves slowly
> there, which is what you
> need. When under attack, fall
> back into the desert, luring your
> enemies into a place where they
> lose all sense of time and space
> and fall under your control.

Authority: To remain disciplined and calm while waiting for disorder to appear amongst the enemy is the art of self-possession.
> —*Sun-tzu (fourth century B.C.)*

Opportunities are changing ceaselessly. Those who get there too early have gone too far, while those who get there too late cannot catch up. As the sun and moon go through their courses, time does not go along with people. Therefore, sages do not value huge jewels as much as they value a little time. Time is hard to find and easy to lose.

HUAINANZI, CHINA, SECOND CENTURY B.C.

OFFENSIVE WARFARE

The greatest dangers in war, and in life, come from the unexpected: people do not respond the way you had thought they would, events mess up your plans and produce confusion, circumstances are overwhelming. In strategy this discrepancy between what you want to happen and what does happen is called "friction." The idea behind conventional offensive warfare is simple: by attacking the other side first, hitting its points of vulnerability, and seizing the initiative and never letting it go, you create your own circumstances. Before any friction can creep in and undermine your plans, you move to the offensive, and your relentless maneuvers force so much friction on the enemy that he collapses.

This is the form of warfare practiced by the most successful captains in history, and the secret to their success is a perfect blend of strategic cleverness and audacity. The strategic element comes in the planning: setting an overall goal, crafting ways to reach it, and thinking the whole plan through in intense detail.

The following eleven chapters will initiate you into this supreme form of warfare. They will help you to put your desires and goals into a larger framework known as "grand strategy." They will show you how to look at your enemies and uncover their secrets. They will describe how a solid base of planning will give you fluid options for attack. Finally, they will show you how to finish off your campaign.

12

LOSE BATTLES BUT WIN THE WAR GRAND STRATEGY

Everyone around you is a strategist angling for power, all trying to promote their own interests, often at your expense. Your daily battles with them make you lose sight of the only thing that really matters: victory in the end, the achievement of greater goals, lasting power. Grand strategy is the art of looking beyond the battle and calculating ahead. It requires that you focus on your ultimate goal and plot to reach it. In grand strategy you consider the political ramifications and long-term consequences of what you do. Instead of reacting emotionally to people, you take control, and make your actions more dimensional, subtle, and effective. Let others get caught up in the twists and turns of the battle, relishing their little victories. Grand strategy will bring you the ultimate reward: the last laugh.

KEYS TO WARFARE

Thousands of years ago, we humans elevated ourselves above the animal world and never looked back. Figuratively speaking, the key to this evolutionary advance was our powers of vision: language, and the ability to reason that it gave us, let us see more of the world around us.

Somewhere along the line, however, we stopped evolving as rational creatures. Despite our progress there is always a part of us that remains animal, and that animal part can respond only to what is most immediate in our environment—it is incapable of thinking beyond the moment. The dilemma affects us still: the two sides of our character, rational and animal, are constantly at war, making almost all of our actions awkward.

More than we are today, the ancient Greeks were close to the passage of the human race from animal to rational. To them our dual nature made us tragic, and the source of tragedy was limited vision.

The Greeks, however, also recognized the potential for a higher human possibility. Those able to see further than others, to control their animal nature and think before they acted, were humans of the most deeply human kind—the ones best able to use the reasoning powers that separate us from animals. As opposed to human stupidity (limited vision), the Greeks imagined an ideal human prudence. Its symbol was Odysseus, who always thought before he acted.

This calm, detached, rational, far-seeing creature, called "prudent" by the Greeks, is what we shall call the "grand strategist."

We are all of us to some extent strategists:

we naturally want control over our lives, and we plot for power, consciously or unconsciously angling to get what we want. We use strategies, in other words, but they tend to be linear and reactive and are often fractured and struck off course by emotional responses. Clever strategists can go far, but all but a few make mistakes. If they are successful, they get carried away and overreach; if they face setbacks—and setbacks are inevitable over a lifetime—they are easily overwhelmed. What sets grand strategists apart is the ability to look more deeply into both themselves and others, to understand and learn from the past and to have a clear sense of the future, to the extent that it can be predicted. Simply, they see more, and their extended vision lets them carry out plans over sometimes-long periods of time.

In a world where people are increasingly incapable of thinking consequentially, more animal than ever, the practice of grand strategy will instantly elevate you above others.

To become a grand strategist does not involve years of study or a total transformation of your personality. It simply means more effective use of what you have—your mind, your rationality, your vision. In ancient times, strategists and historians from Suntzu to Thucydides became conscious of this recurring self-destructive pattern in warfare and began to work out more rational ways to fight. The first step was to think beyond the immediate battle. Supposing you won victory, where would it leave you—better off or worse? To answer that question, the logical step was to think ahead, to the third and fourth battles on, which connected like links

SELECTED MILITARY WRITINGS, MAO TSE-TUNG, 1893–1976

in a chain. The result was the concept of the campaign, in which the strategist sets a realistic goal and plots several steps ahead to get there. Individual battles matter only in the way they set up the next ones down the line; an army can even deliberately lose a battle as part of a long-term plan. The victory that matters is that of the overall campaign, and everything is subordinated to that goal.

Military history shows that the key to grand strategy—the thing that separates it from simple, garden-variety strategy—is its particular quality of forethought. Grand strategists think and plan further into the future before taking action. Nor is their planning simply a matter of accumulating knowledge and information; it involves looking at the world with a dispassionate eye, thinking in terms of the campaign, planning indirect, subtle steps along the way whose purpose may only gradually become visible to others. Not only does this kind of planning fool and disorient the enemy; for the strategist it has the psychological effects of calm, a sense of perspective, flexibility to change in the moment while keeping the ultimate goal in mind.

Grand strategy has four main principles, outlined below. The more you can incorporate these principles into your plans, the better the results.

Focus on your greater goal, your destiny. The first step toward becoming a grand strategist—the step that will make everything else fall into place—is to begin with a clear, detailed, purposeful goal in mind, one rooted in reality. We often imagine that we generally operate by some kind of plan, that we have goals we are trying to reach. But we're usually fooling ourselves; what we have are not goals but wishes. What have distinguished all history's grand strategists and can distinguish you, too, are specific, detailed, focused goals. Clear long-term objectives give direction to all of your actions, large and small. Important decisions become easier to make.

Your goals must be rooted in reality. If they are simply beyond your means, essentially impossible for you to realize, you will grow discouraged, and discouragement can quickly escalate into a defeatist attitude. On the other hand, if your goals lack a certain dimension and grandeur, it can be hard to stay motivated. Do not be afraid to be bold.

Widen your perspective. Grand strategy is a function of vision, of seeing further in time and space than the enemy does. The process of foresight is unnatural: we can only ever live in the present. Your task as a grand strategist is to force yourself to widen your view, to take in more of the world around you, to see things for what they are and for how they may play out in the future, not for how you wish them to be.

You can take a step in this direction by always trying to look at the world through the eyes of other people—including, most definitely, your enemy—before engaging in war. Your own cultural preconceptions are a major hindrance to seeing the world objectively.

Grand strategists keep sensitive antennae attuned to the politics of any situation. Politics is the art of promoting and

THE WILD BOAR AND THE FOX

A wild boar was sharpening his tusks on a tree trunk one day. A fox asked him why he did this when there was neither huntsman nor danger threatening him. "I do so for a good reason," he replied. "For if I am suddenly surprised by danger I wouldn't have the time to sharpen my tusks. But now I will find them ready to do their duty."

The fable shows that it is no good waiting until danger comes to be ready.

FABLES, AESOP, SIXTH CENTURY B.C.

protecting your own interests. Your behavior in the world always has political consequences, in that the people around you will analyze it in terms of whether it helps or harms them.

Taking politics into account, you must figure out your grand strategy with a mind to gaining support from other people—to creating and strengthening a base. Being political means understanding people—seeing through their eyes.

Sever the roots. In a society dominated by appearances, the real source of a problem is sometimes hard to grasp. To work out a grand strategy against an enemy, you have to know what motivates him or is the source of his power. Too many wars and battles drag on because neither side knows how to strike at the other's roots. As a grand strategist, you must expand your vision not only far and wide but under. Think hard, dig deep, do not take appearances for reality. Uncover the roots of the trouble and you can strategize to sever them, ending the war or problem with finality.

Take the indirect route to your goal. The greatest danger you face in strategy is losing the initiative and finding yourself constantly reacting to what the other side does. The solution, of course, is to plan ahead but also to plan subtly—to take the indirect route. Preventing your opponent from seeing the purpose of your actions gives you an enormous advantage.

Always pay attention to the first step of the campaign. It sets the tempo, determines the enemy's mind-set, and launches you in a direction that had better be the right one.

Whenever anything goes wrong, it is human nature to blame this person or that. When an action goes wrong—in business, in politics, in life—trace it back to the policy that inspired it in the first place. The goal was misguided.

This means that you yourself are largely the agent of anything bad that happens to you. With more prudence, wiser policies, and greater vision, you could have avoided the danger. So when something goes wrong, look deep into yourself to make sure that you start your next campaign with a firmer step and greater vision.

Image:
The Mountaintop.
Down on the battle-
field, everything is
smoke and confusion. It is
hard to tell friend from foe,
to see who is winning, to
foresee the enemy's next move. The
general must climb high above the fray,
to the mountaintop, where everything
becomes clearer and more in focus. There he
can see beyond the battlefield—to the movements of
reserves, to the enemy camp, to the battle's future shape.
Only from the mountaintop can the general direct the war.

Authority: It is a common mistake in going to war to begin at the wrong end, to act first and to wait for disaster to discuss the matter. —*Thucydides (between 460 and 455 B.C.–circa 400 B.C.)*

13

KNOW YOUR ENEMY
THE INTELLIGENCE
STRATEGY

The target of your strategies should be less the army you face than the mind of the man or woman who runs it. If you understand how that mind works, you have the key to deceiving and controlling it. Train yourself to read people, picking up the signals they unconsciously send about their innermost thoughts and intentions. A friendly front will let you watch them closely and mine them for information. Beware of projecting your own emotions and mental habits onto them; try to think as they think. By finding your opponents' psychological weaknesses, you can work to unhinge their minds.

He who knows the enemy and himself Will never in a hundred battles be at risk.

SUN-TZU, FOURTH CENTURY B.C.

Anger as spy.—Anger empties out the soul and brings even its dregs to light. That is why, if we know no other way of discovering the truth of the matter, we must know how to put our acquaintances, our adherents and opponents, into a rage, so as to learn all that is really being thought and undertaken against us.

HUMAN, ALL TOO HUMAN, FRIEDRICH NIETZSCHE, 1886

The greatest power you could have in life would come neither from limitless resources nor even consummate skill in strategy. It would come from clear knowledge of those around you—the ability to read people like a book. Given that knowledge, you could distinguish friend from foe, smoking out snakes in the grass.

This kind of knowledge has been a military goal since the dawn of history. That is why the arts of intelligence gathering and spying were invented. But spies are unreliable; they filter information through their own preconceptions and prejudices, and the nuances that give people away—the tone in a speaker's voice, the look in his or her eyes—are inevitably missing from their reports. In the end the spy's information means nothing unless you are adept at interpreting human behavior and psychology. Without that skill you will see in it what you want to see, confirming your own prejudices. The leaders who have made best use of intelligence were all first and foremost great students of human nature and superior readers of men. They honed their skills through personal observation of people. Only with that foundation could the use of spies extend their powers of vision.

The first step in the process is to get over the idea that people are impenetrable mysteries and that only some trick will let you peek into their souls. If they seem mysterious, it is because almost all of us learn to disguise our true feelings and intentions from an early age. If we went around showing just how we felt and telling people what we planned to do, we would make ourselves vulnerable to malice, and if we always spoke our minds, we would offend a lot of people unnecessarily. So as we grow up, concealing much of what we are thinking becomes second nature.

This deliberate opacity makes the intelligence game difficult but not impossible. For even as people consciously struggle to conceal what is going on in their minds, they unconsciously want to reveal themselves.

Understand: day in and day out, people emit signals that reveal their intentions and deepest desires. If we do not pick them up, it is because we are not paying attention. You will be amazed at how much you can pick up about people if you can shut off your incessant interior monologue, empty your thoughts, and anchor yourself in the moment.

It is of course critical that people be unaware you are watching them so closely. A friendly front will help disguise what you're doing. Do not ask too many questions; the trick is to get people to relax and open up without prodding, shadowing them so quietly that they never guess what you're really up to.

Information is useless unless you know how to interpret it, how to use it to tell appearance from reality. You must learn how to recognize a range of psychological types. Be alert, for instance, to the phenomenon of the masked opposite: when someone strikingly manifests a particular personality trait, that trait may well be a cover-up.

In general, it is easier to observe people in action, particularly in moments of crisis. Those are the times when they either reveal their weakness or struggle so hard to disguise it that you can see through the mask.

In my opinion, there are two kinds of eyes: one kind simply looks at things and the other sees through things to perceive their inner nature. The former should not be tense [so as to observe as much as possible]; the latter should be strong [so as to discern the workings of the opponent's mind clearly]. Sometimes a man can read another's mind with his eyes. In fencing, it is all right to allow your own eyes to express your will but never let them reveal your mind. This matter should be considered carefully and studied diligently.

MIYAMOTO
MUSASHI,
1584–1645

The quality of the information you gather on your enemies is more important than the quantity. A single but crucial nugget can be the key to their destruction.

There are, of course, limits to how much intelligence gathering you can achieve by firsthand observation. A network of spies will extend your vision, particularly as you learn to interpret the information they bring you. An informal network is the best—a group of allies recruited over time to be your eyes and ears. Try to make friends with people at or near the source of information on your rival; one well-placed friend will yield far more than will a handful of paid spies.

Always look for internal spies, people in the enemy camp who are dissatisfied and have an ax to grind. Turn them to your purposes and they will give you better information than any infiltrator you sneak in from outside. Hire people the enemy has fired— they will tell you how the enemy thinks. A warning: never rely on one spy, one source of information, no matter how good. You risk being played or getting slanted, one-sided information.

Many people leave a paper trail of writings, interviews, and so on that is as revealing as anything you can learn from a spy. People reveal a lot about themselves in their writing.

Finally, the enemy you are dealing with is not an inanimate object that will simply respond in an expected manner to your strategies. Your enemies are constantly changing and adapting to what you are doing. Innovating and inventing on their own, they try to learn from their mistakes and from your successes. So your knowledge of the enemy cannot be static. Keep your intelligence up to date, and do not rely on the enemy's responding the same way twice.

Image: The Shadow. Everyone has a shadow, a secret self, a dark side. This shadow comprises everything people try to hide from the world—their weaknesses, secret desires, selfish intentions. This shadow is invisible from a distance; to see it you must get up close, physically and most of all psychologically. Then it will come into relief. Follow close in your target's footsteps and he will not notice how much of his shadow he has revealed.

Authority: Thus the reason the farsighted ruler and his superior commander conquer the enemy at every move, and achieve successes far beyond the reach of the common crowd, is advance knowledge. Such knowledge cannot be had from ghosts and spirits, educed by comparison with past events, or verified by astrological calculations. It must come from people—people who know the enemy's situation. —*Sun-tzu (fourth century B.C.)*

14

OVERWHELM RESISTANCE WITH SPEED AND SUDDENNESS
THE BLITZKRIEG STRATEGY

In a world in which many people are indecisive and overly cautious, the use of speed will bring you untold power. Striking first, before your opponents have time to think or prepare, will make them emotional, unbalanced, and prone to error. When you follow with another swift and sudden maneuver, you will induce further panic and confusion. This strategy works best with a setup, a lull—your unexpected action catches your enemy off guard. When you strike, hit with unrelenting force. Acting with speed and decisiveness will garner you respect, awe, and irresistible momentum.

*The hexagram
Chen represents
the eldest son,
who seizes rule
with energy and
power. A yang
line develops
below two yin
lines and presses
upward forcibly.
This movement
is so violent that
it arouses terror.
It is symbolized
by thunder,
which bursts
forth from the
earth and by its
shock causes fear
and trembling.*

*THE
JUDGEMENT
SHOCK brings
success. Shock
comes—oh, oh!
Laughing
words— ha,
ha! The shock
terrifies for
a hundred
miles. . . .*

THE I CHING,
CHINA, CIRCA
EIGHTH CENTURY
B.C.

KEYS TO WARFARE

In May 1940 the German army invaded France and the Low Countries using a new form of warfare: the blitzkrieg. Advancing with incredible speed, the Germans coordinated tanks and airplanes in an attack that culminated in one of the quickest and most devastating victories in military history. The success of the blitzkrieg was largely due to the Allies' static, rigid defense. When the Germans breached this defense, the Allies could not adjust or react in time.

Now more than ever, we find ourselves dealing with people who are defensive and cautious, who begin any action from a static position. The reason is simple: the pace of modern life is increasingly growing faster, full of distractions, annoyances, and interruptions. The natural response for many is to retreat inward, to erect psychological walls against the harsh realities of modern life.

Blitzkrieg warfare, adapted for daily combat, is the perfect strategy for these times. While those around you remain defensive and immobile, you surprise them with sudden and decisive action, forcing them to act before they are ready. They cannot respond, as they usually do, by being elusive or cautious. They will most likely become emotional and react imprudently. You have breached their defenses, and if you keep up the pressure and hit them again with something unexpected, you will send them into a kind of downward psychological spiral—pushing them into mistakes, which further deepens their confusion, and so the cycle goes on.

In launching a blitzkrieg, you must begin by finding your enemy's weak point.

Initiating the action where there will be less resistance will allow you to develop crucial momentum. Speed is not only a powerful tool to use against an enemy, but it can also have a bracing, positive influence on those on your side. Velocity creates a sense of vitality. Moving with speed means there is less time for you and your army to make mistakes. It also creates a bandwagon effect: more and more people admiring your boldness, will decide to join forces with you.

War is such that the supreme consideration is speed. This is to take advantage of what is beyond the reach of the enemy, to go by way of routes where he least expects you, and to attack where he has made no preparations.

SUN-TZU, FOURTH CENTURY B.C.

Veni, vidi, vici (I came, I saw, I conquered).

JULIUS CAESAR, 100–44 B.C.

Image: The Storm. The sky becomes still and calm, and a lull sets in, peaceful and soothing. Then, out of nowhere, lightning strikes, the wind picks up . . . and the sky explodes. It is the suddenness of the storm that is so terrifying.

Authority: You must be slow in deliberation and swift in execution. —*Napoleon Bonaparte (1769–1821)*

15

CONTROL THE DYNAMIC FORCING STRATEGIES

People are constantly struggling to control you—getting you to act in their interests, keeping the dynamic on their terms. The only way to get the upper hand is to make your play for control more intelligent and insidious. Instead of trying to dominate the other side's every move, work to define the nature of the relationship itself. Shift the conflict to terrain of your choice, altering the pace and stakes to suit you. Maneuver to control your opponents' minds, pushing their emotional buttons, and compelling them to make mistakes. If necessary, let them feel they are in control in order to get them to lower their guard. If you control the overall direction and framing of the battle, anything they do will play into your hands.

THE ART OF ULTIMATE CONTROL

Control is an issue in all relationships. It is human nature to abhor feelings of helplessness and to strive for power. Whenever two people or groups interact, there is a constant maneuvering between them to define the relationship, to determine who has control over this and that. This battle of wills is inevitable. Your task as a strategist is twofold: First, recognize the struggle for control in all aspects of life, and never be taken in by those who claim they are not interested in control. Such types are often the most manipulative of all. Second, you must master the art of moving the other side like pieces on a chessboard, with purpose and direction. This art was cultivated by the most creative generals and military strategists throughout the ages.

War is above all else a struggle over who can control the actions of the other side to a greater extent. Military geniuses such as Hannibal, Napoleon, and Erwin Rommel discovered that the best way to attain control is to determine the overall pace, direction, and shape of the war itself. This means getting enemies to fight according to your tempo, luring them onto terrain that is unfamiliar to them and suited to you, playing to your strengths. And, most important of all, it means gaining influence over the frame of mind of your opponents, adapting your maneuvers to their psychological weaknesses.

The superior strategist understands that it is impossible to control exactly how an enemy will respond to this move or that. To attempt to do so will only lead to frustration and exhaustion. There is too much in war and in life that is unpredictable. But if the strategist can control the mood and mind-set of his enemies, it does not matter exactly how they respond to his maneuvers. If he can make them frightened, panicky, overly aggressive, and angry, he controls the wider scope of their actions and can trap them mentally before cornering them physically.

Control can be aggressive or passive. It can be an immediate push on the enemy, making him back up and lose the initiative. It can be playing possum, getting the enemy to lower his guard, or baiting him into a rash attack. The artist of control weaves both of these into a devastating pattern—hitting, backing off, baiting, overwhelming.

This art is infinitely applicable to the battles of everyday life. Many people tend to play unconscious games of domination or get caught up in trying to control someone else's every move. In trying to manage and determine too much, they exhaust them-selves, make mistakes, push people away, and in the end lose control of the situation. If you understand and master the art, you will instantly become more creative in your approach to influencing and controlling the other side. By determining people's moods, the pace at which they must move, the stakes involved, you will find that almost anything people do in response to your maneuvers will fit into the overall dynamic you have shaped. They may know they are being controlled but be helpless to fight it, or they may move in the direction you desire without realizing it. That is ultimate control.

The following are the four basic prin-ciples of the art.

*In short, I think
like Frederick
[the Great], one
should always be
the first to attack.*

NAPOLEON
BONAPARTE,
1769–1821

Keep them on their heels. Before the enemy makes a move, before the element of chance or the unexpected actions of your opponents can ruin your plans, you make an aggressive move to seize the initiative. You then keep up a relentless pressure, exploiting this momentary advantage to the fullest. You do not wait for opportunities to open up; you make them yourself. If you are the weaker side, this will often more than level the playing field. Keeping your enemies on the defensive and in react mode will have a demoralizing effect on them.

Shift the battlefield. An enemy naturally wants to fight you on familiar terrain. Terrain in this sense means all of the details of the battle—the time and place, exactly what is being fought over, who is involved in the struggle, and so on. By subtly shifting your enemies into places and situations that are not familiar to them, you control the dynamic. Without realizing what is happening, your opponents find themselves fighting on your terms.

Compel mistakes. Your enemies depend on executing a strategy that plays to their advantages, that has worked in the past. Your task is twofold: to fight the battle in such a way that they cannot bring their strength or strategy into play and to create such a level of frustration that they make mistakes in the process. You do not give them enough time to do anything; you play to their emotional weaknesses, making them as irritable as possible; you bait them into deadly traps. It is less your action than their missteps that give you control.

Assume passive control. The ultimate form of domination is to make those on the other side think they are the ones in control. Believing they are in command, they are less likely to resist you or become defensive. You create this impression by moving with the energy of the other side, giving ground but slowly and subtly diverting them in the direction you desire. It is often the best way to control the overly aggressive and the passive-aggressive.

Given the same amount of intelligence, timidity will do a thousand times more damage in war than audacity.

CARL VON CLAUSEWITZ, 1780–1831

Image: The Boxer. The superior fighter does not rely on his powerful punch or quick reflexes. Instead he creates a rhythm to the fight that suits him, advancing and retreating at a pace he sets; he controls the ring, moving his opponent to the center, to the ropes, toward or away from him. Master of time and space, he creates frustration, compels mistakes, and engenders a mental collapse that precedes the physical. He wins not with his fists but by controlling the ring.

Authority: In order to have rest oneself it is necessary to keep the enemy occupied. This throws them back on the defensive, and once they are placed that way they cannot rise up again during the entire campaign. —*Frederick the Great (1712–1786)*

16

HIT THEM WHERE IT HURTS
THE CENTER-OF-GRAVITY
STRATEGY

Everyone has a source of power on which he or she depends. When you look at your rivals, search below the surface for that source, the center of gravity that holds the entire structure together. That center can be their wealth, their popularity, a key position, a winning strategy. Hitting them there will inflict disproportionate pain. Find what the other side most cherishes and protects—that is where you must strike.

The third shogun Iemitsu was fond of sword matches. Once, when he arranged to see some of his outstanding swordsmen display their skills, he spotted among the gathering a master equestrian by the name of Suwa Bunkuro, and impulsively asked him to take part. Bunkuro responded by saying that he would be pleased to if he could fight on horseback, adding that he could defeat anyone on horseback. Iemitsu was delighted to urge the swordsmen to fight Bunkuro in the style he preferred. As it turned out, Bunkuro was right in his boasting. Brandishing a sword on a prancing horse wasn't something many

It is natural in war to focus on the physical aspect of conflict—bodies, equipment, matériel. Even an enlightened strategist will tend to look first at the enemy's army, firepower, mobility, reserves. War is a visceral, emotional affair, an arena of physical danger, and it takes great effort to rise above this level and ask different questions: What makes the enemy army move? What gives it impetus and endurance? Who guides its actions? What is the underlying source of its strength?

It is the nature of power to present a forceful front, to seem menacing and intimidating, strong and decisive. But this outward display is often exaggerated or even downright deceptive, since power does not dare show its weaknesses. And beneath the display is the support on which power rests.

To attack this center of gravity, to neutralize or destroy it, is the ultimate strategy in war, for without it the whole structure will collapse. Hitting the center will have devastating psychological effects, throwing the enemy off balance and inducing a creeping panic. If conventional generals look at the physical aspect of the enemy army, focusing on its weaknesses and trying to exploit them, superior strategists look behind and beyond, to the support system. The enemy's center of gravity is where an injury will hurt him most, his point of greatest vulnerability. Hitting him there is the best way to end the conflict definitively and economically.

To find a group's center of gravity, you must understand its structure and the culture within which it operates. If your enemies are individuals, you must fathom their psychology, what makes them tick, the structure of their thinking and priorities.

The more centralized the enemy, the more devastating becomes a blow at its leader or governing body. A more decentralized enemy will have several separate centers of gravity. The key here is to disorganize them by cutting off communication between them; if the parts cannot communicate with the whole, chaos ensues.

In any interaction with people, you must train yourself to focus on their strength, the source of their power, whatever it is that gives them their most crucial support. That knowledge will afford you many strategic options, many angles from which to attack, subtly or not so subtly undermining their strength rather than hitting it head-on. You can create no greater sense of panic in your enemies than that of being unable to use their strengths.

> **Image:** The Wall. Your opponents stand behind a wall, which protects them from strangers and intruders. Do not hit your head against the wall or lay siege to it; find the pillars and supports that make it stand and give it strength. Dig under the wall, sapping its foundations until it collapses on its own.

swordsmen were used to, and Bunkuro easily defeated everyone who dared face him on horseback. Somewhat exasperated, Iemitsu told Munenori to give it a try. Though a bystander on this occasion, Munenori at once complied and mounted a horse. As his horse trotted up to Bunkuro's, Munenori suddenly stopped his horse and slapped the nose of Bunkuro's horse with his wooden sword. Bunkuro's horse reared, and while the famed equestrian was trying to restore his balance, Munenori struck him off his horse.

THE SWORD AND THE MIND, TRANS BY HIROAKI SATO, 1985

Man depends on his throat for fluent breathing and the maintenance of life. When his throat is strangled, his five sense organs will lose their sensibility and no longer function normally. He will not be able to stretch his limbs, which become numb and paralyzed. The man can therefore rarely survive. Thus, when the banners of the enemy come into sight and the beating of its battle drums can be heard, we must first ascertain the positions of its back and throat. Then we can attack it from the back and strangle its throat.

THE WILES OF WAR: 36 MILITARY STRATEGIES FROM ANCIENT CHINA, TRANS SUN HAICHEN, 1991

Authority: The first principle is that the ultimate substance of enemy strength must be traced back to the fewest possible sources, and ideally to one alone. The attack on these sources must be compressed into the fewest possible actions.... By constantly seeking out the center of his power, by daring all to win all, will one really defeat the enemy.

—*Carl von Clausewitz, On War (1780–1831)*

17

DEFEAT THEM IN DETAIL THE DIVIDE-AND-CONQUER STRATEGY

When you look at your enemies, do not be intimidated by their appearance. Instead look at the parts that make up the whole. By separating the parts, sowing dissension and division from within, you can weaken and bring down even the most formidable foe. In setting up your attack, work on their minds to create internal conflict. Look for the joints and links, the things that connect the people in a group or connect one group to another. Division is weakness, and the joints are the weakest part of any structure. When you are facing troubles or enemies, turn a large problem into small, eminently defeatable parts.

THE THREE
OXEN AND THE
LION

*There were three
oxen who always
grazed together.
A lion had his
designs upon
them and wanted
to eat them, but
he could never
get at one of
them because
they were always
together. So he
set them against
each other with
slanderous talk
and managed
to get them
separated,
whereupon they
were isolated
and he was able
to eat them one
after the other.*

FABLES, AESOP,
SIXTH CENTURY
B.C.

KEYS TO WARFARE

Lurking deep in even the most civilized among us is the basic fear of being alone, unsupported, and exposed to danger. People today are more dispersed and society is less cohesive than ever before, but that only increases our need to belong to a group, to have a strong network of allies—to feel supported and protected on all sides. Take away this feeling and we are returned to a primitive sensation of terror at our own vulnerability. The divide-and-conquer strategy has never been more effective than it is today: cut people off from their group—make them feel alienated, alone, and unprotected—and you weaken them enormously. That moment of weakness gives you great power to maneuver them into a corner, whether to seduce or to induce panic and retreat.

Before you launch an outright attack on your enemies, it is always wise first to weaken them by creating as much division in their ranks as possible. One good place to drive a wedge is between the leadership and the people, whether soldiers or citizenry; leaders function poorly when they lose their support among the people.

Divide and rule is a powerful strategy for governing any group. It is based on a key principle: within any organization people naturally form smaller groups based on mutual self-interest—the primitive desire to find strength in numbers. These subgroups form power bases that, left unchecked, will threaten the organization as a whole. The formation of parties and factions can be a leader's greatest threat, for in time these factions will naturally work to secure their own interests before those of the greater group. The solution is to divide to rule. To do so you must first establish yourself as the center of power; individuals must know they need to compete for your approval. There has to be more to be gained by pleasing the leader than by trying to form a power base within the group.

Think of the people in your group who are working primarily for their own interests as insurgents. They thrive on discontent in the organization, fanning it into dissension and factionalism. You can always work to divide such factions once you know about them, but the better solution is to keep your soldiers satisfied and contented, giving the insurgents nothing to feed on. Bitter and isolated, they will die off on their own.

The most important thing is to move quickly against your enemies. Waiting for troubles to come to you will only multiply them and give them a deadly momentum.

Every kingdom divided against itself is laid waste, and a divided household falls. And if Satan also is divided against himself, how will his kingdom stand?

LUKE 11:14

Image: The Knot. It is large, hopelessly entangled, and seemingly impossible to unravel. The knot consists of thousands of smaller knots, all twisted and intertwined. Let time go by and the knot will get only worse. Instead of trying to pick it apart from this side or that, take up your sword and cut it in half with one blow. Once divided, it will come undone on its own.

Authority: In antiquity those who were referred to as excelling in the employment of the army were able to keep the enemy's forward and rear forces from connecting; the many and few from relying on each other;

the noble and lowly from coming to each other's rescue; the upper and lower ranks from trusting each other; the troops to be separated, unable to reassemble, or when assembled, not to be well-ordered. —*Sun-tzu (fourth century B.C.)*

18

EXPOSE AND ATTACK YOUR OPPONENT'S SOFT FLANK THE TURNING STRATEGY

When you attack people directly, you stiffen their resistance and make your task that much harder. There is a better way: distract your opponents' attention to the front, then attack them from the side, where they least expect it. By hitting them where they are soft, tender, and unprotected, you create a shock, a moment of weakness for you to exploit. Bait people into going out on a limb, exposing their weakness, then rake them with fire from the side. The only way to get stubborn opponents to move is to approach them indirectly.

*Your gentleness
shall force
More than your
force move us
to gentleness.*

As You Like
It, William
Shakespeare,
1564–1616

The Book of
Changes (I
Ching) *is often
considered
the Oriental
apotheosis of
adaptation,
of flexibility.
In this book
the recurring
theme is one of
observing life
and blending
with its flow in
order to survive
and develop. In
effect, the theme
of this work is
that everything
in existence
can be a source
of conflict, of
danger, and,
ultimately,
of violence if
opposed from
the wrong angle
or in the wrong
manner—that
is, if confronted
directly at*

The people who win true power in the difficult modern world are those who have
learned indirection. They know the value
of approaching at an angle, disguising their
intentions, lowering the enemy's resistance,
hitting the soft, exposed flank instead of butt-
ing horns. Rather than try to push or pull
people, they coax them to turn in the direction they desire. This takes effort but pays
dividends down the road in reduced conflict
and greater results.

Never reveal your intentions or goals;
instead use charm, pleasant conversation,
humor, flattery—whatever works—to hold
people's attention to the front. Their focus
elsewhere, their flank is exposed, and now
when you drop hints or suggest subtle
changes in direction, the gates are open and
the walls are down. They are disarmed and
maneuverable.

Think of people's ego and vanity as a kind
of front. When they are attacking you and you
don't know why, it is often because you have
inadvertently threatened their ego, their sense
of importance in the world. Whenever possible, you must work to make people feel secure
about themselves. Again, use whatever works:
subtle flattery, a gift, an unexpected promo-
tion, an offer of alliance, a presentation of you
and they as equals, a mirroring of their ideas
and values. All these things will make them
feel anchored in their frontal position relative
to the world, lowering their defenses and making them like you. Secure and comfortable,
they are now set up for a flanking maneuver.
This is particularly devastating with a target
whose ego is delicate.

A common way of using the flanking maneuver in war is to get your enemies to expose themselves on a weak salient. This means maneuvering them onto ground or luring them to advance in such a way that their front is narrow and their flanks are long—a delicious target for a side attack.

When people present their ideas and arguments, they often censor themselves, trying to appear more conciliatory and flexible than is actually the case. If you attack them directly from the front, you end up not getting very far, because there isn't much there to aim at. Instead try to make them go further with their ideas, giving you a bigger target. Do this by standing back, seeming to go along, and baiting them into moving rashly ahead. They will expose themselves on a weak salient, advancing an indefensible argument or position that will make them look ridiculous. The key is never to strike too early. Give your opponents time to hang themselves.

In a political world, people are dependent on their social position. They need support from as many sources as possible. That support, the base of most people's power, presents a rich flank to expose and attack. A flanking attack on someone's social status and reputation will make him or her turn to face this menace, giving you ample room to maneuver the opponent in other directions. The more subtle and indirect your maneuvers in life, the better. The ultimate evolution of strategy is toward more and more indirection. An opponent who cannot see where you are heading is at a severe disadvantage. The more angles you use the harder it will be for your opponents to defend themselves.

the point of its maximum strength, since this approach renders the encounter potentially devastating. By the same token, any and every occurrence can be dealt with by approaching it from the right angle and in the proper manner— that is, at its source, before it can develop full power, or from the sides (the vulnerable "flanks of a tiger").

SECRETS OF THE SAMURAI, OSCAR RATTI AND ADELE WESTBROOK, 1973

Image: The Lobster. The creature seems intimidating
and impenetrable, with its sharp claws quick to grab,
its hard protective shell, its powerful tail propelling
it out of danger. Handle it directly and you will
pay the price. But turn it over with a stick
to reveal its tender underside and
the creature is rendered
helpless.

Authority: It is by turning the enemy, by attacking his
flank, that battles are won. —*Napoleon Bonaparte (1769–1821)*

19

ENVELOP THE ENEMY
THE ANNIHILATION
STRATEGY

People will use any kind of gap in your defenses to attack you or revenge themselves on you. So offer no gaps. The secret is to envelop your opponents—create relentless pressure on them from all sides, dominate their attention, and close off their access to the outside world. Make your attacks unpredictable to create a vaporous feeling of vulnerability. Finally, as you sense their weakening resolve, crush their willpower by tightening the noose. The best encirclements are psychological—you have surrounded their minds.

You must make
your opponent
acknowledge
defeat from
the bottom of
his heart.

MIYAMOTO
MUSASHI
(1584–1645)

KEYS TO WARFARE

Thousands of years ago, we humans lived a nomadic life, wandering across deserts and plains, hunting and gathering. Then we shifted into living in settlements and cultivating our food. The change brought us comfort and control, but in a part of our spirit we remain nomads: we cannot help but associate the room to roam and wander with a feeling of freedom. Over the centuries this reflex has become more psychological: the feeling that we have options in a situation, a future with prospects, translates into something like the feeling of open space. Our minds thrive on the sense that there is possibility and strategic room to maneuver.

Conversely, the sense of psychological enclosure is deeply disturbing to us, often making us overreact. When someone or something encircles us—narrowing our options, besieging us from all sides—we lose control of our emotions and make the kinds of mistakes that render the situation more hopeless.

The battles of daily life occur not on a map but in a kind of abstract space defined by people's ability to maneuver, act against you, limit your power, and cut into your time to respond. Give your opponents any room in this abstract or psychological space and they will exploit it, no matter how powerful you are or how brilliant your strategies—so make them feel surrounded. Shrink their possibilities of action and close off their escape routes. Just as the inhabitants of a city under siege may slowly lose their minds, your opponents will be maddened by their lack of room to maneuver against you.

To envelop your enemies, you must use whatever you have in abundance. If you have a large army, use it to create the appearance that your forces are everywhere, an encircling pressure.

Remember: the power of envelopment is ultimately psychological. Making the other side *feel* vulnerable to attack on many sides is as good as enveloping them physically.

A few well-timed blows to make your enemies feel vulnerable in multiple ways and from multiple directions will do the same thing for you. Often, in fact, less is more here: too many blows will give you a shape, a personality—something for the other side to respond to and develop a strategy to combat. Instead, seem vaporous. Make your maneuvers impossible to anticipate. Your psychological encirclement will be all the more sinister and complete.

The best encirclements are those that prey on the enemy's preexisting, inherent vulnerabilities. Be attentive, then, to signs of arrogance, rashness, or other psychological weakness. Feed the fears of the paranoid and they will start to imagine attacks you hadn't even thought of; their overheated brains will do much of the encirclement for you.

The impetuous, violent, and arrogant are particularly easy to lure into the traps of envelopment strategies: play weak or dumb and they will charge ahead without stopping to think where they're going. But any emotional weakness on the opponent's part, or any great desire or unrealized wish, can be made an ingredient of encirclement. In luring your enemies into such a trap, always try to make them feel as if they are in control of the situation. They will advance as far as you want them to.

Finally, do not simply work to envelop your opponents' forces or immediate emotions, but rather envelop their whole strategy—indeed, their whole conceptual framework. This ultimate form of envelopment involves first studying the rigid, predictable parts of your opponents' strategy, then crafting a novel strategy of your own that goes outside their experience. This kind of strategic mismatch can lead to victory not just in any given battle but in large-scale campaigns—the ultimate goal in any form of war.

Image:
The Noose. Once it is in place, there is no escape, no hope. At the mere thought of being caught in it, the enemy will grow desperate and struggle, its frantic efforts to escape only hastening its destruction.

Authority: Place a monkey in a cage, and it is the same as a pig, not because it isn't clever and quick, but because it has no place to freely exercise its capabilities. —*Huainanzi (second century B.C.)*

20

MANEUVER THEM INTO WEAKNESS
THE RIPENING-FOR-THE-SICKLE STRATEGY

No matter how strong you are, fighting endless battles with people is exhausting, costly, and unimaginative. Wise strategists generally prefer the art of maneuver: before the battle even begins, they find ways to put their opponents in positions of such weakness that victory is easy and quick. Bait enemies into taking positions that may seem alluring but are actually traps and blind alleys. If their position is strong, get them to abandon it by leading them on a wild-goose chase. Create dilemmas: devise maneuvers that give them a choice of ways to respond—all of them bad. Channel chaos and disorder in their direction. Confused, frustrated, and angry opponents are like ripe fruit on the bough: the slightest breeze will make them fall.

Warfare is like hunting. Wild animals are taken by scouting, by nets, by lying in wait, by stalking, by circling around, and by other such stratagems rather than by sheer force. In waging war we should proceed in the same way, whether the enemy be many or few. To try simply to overpower the enemy in the open, hand to hand and face to face, even though you might appear to win, is an enterprise which is very risky and can result in serious harm. Apart from extreme emergency, it is ridiculous to try to gain a victory which is so costly and brings only empty glory....

BYZANTINE
EMPEROR
MAURIKIOS,
A.D. 539–602

MANEUVER WARFARE

Throughout history two distinct styles of warfare can be identified. The most ancient is the war of attrition: the enemy surrenders because you have killed so many of its men. A general fighting a war of attrition will calculate ways to overwhelm the other side with larger numbers, or with the battle formation that will do the most damage, or with superior military technology. In any event, victory depends on wearing down the other side in battle. Even with today's extraordinary technology, attrition warfare is remarkably unsophisticated, playing into humanity's most violent instincts.

Over many centuries, and most notably in ancient China, a second method of waging war developed. The emphasis here was not destroying the other side in battle but weakening and unbalancing it before the battle began. The leader would maneuver to confuse and infuriate and to put the enemy in a bad position—having to fight uphill, or with the sun or wind in its face, or in a cramped space. In this kind of war, an army with mobility could be more effective than one with muscle.

The maneuver-warfare philosophy was codified by Sun-tzu in his *Art of War*, written in China's Warring States period, in the fifth to third century B.C.—over two hundred years of escalating cycles of warfare in which a state's very survival depended on its army and strategists. To Sun-tzu and his contemporaries, it was obvious that the costs of war went far beyond its body counts: it entailed a loss of resources and political goodwill and a lowering of morale among soldiers and citizens. These costs would mount over time until eventually even the greatest warrior nation would succumb to exhaustion. But through adroit maneuvering a state could spare itself such high costs and still emerge victorious. An enemy who had been maneuvered into a weak position would succumb more easily to psychological pressure; even before the battle had begun, it had imperceptibly started to collapse and would surrender with less of a fight.

Several strategists outside Asia—most notably Napoleon Bonaparte—have made brilliant use of maneuver warfare. But in general, attrition warfare is deeply engrained in the Western way of thinking—from the ancient Greeks to modern America. In an attrition culture, thoughts naturally gravitate toward how to overpower problems, obstacles, those who resist us. In the media, emphasis is placed on big battles, whether in politics or in the arts—static situations in which there are winners and losers. People are drawn to the emotional and dramatic quality in any confrontation, not the many steps that lead to such confrontation. The stories that are told in such cultures are all geared toward such battlelike moments, a moral message preached through the ending (as opposed to the more telling details). On top of it all, this way of fighting is deemed more manly, honorable, honest.

More than anything, maneuver war is a different way of thinking. What matters here is process—the steps toward battle and how to manipulate them to make the confrontation less costly and violent. In the maneuver universe, nothing is static. Battles are in

Aptitude for maneuver is the supreme skill in a general; it is the most useful and rarest of gifts by which genius is estimated.

NAPOLEON BONAPARTE, 1769–1821

Now the army's disposition of force (hsing) *is like water. Water's configuration* (hsing) *avoids heights and races downward.... Water configures* (hsing) *its flow in accord with the terrain; the army controls its victory in accord with the enemy. Thus the army does not maintain any constant strategic configuration of power* (shih), *water has no constant shape* (hsing). *One who is able to change and transform in accord with the enemy and wrest victory is termed spiritual.*

THE ART OF WAR,
SUN-TZU, FOURTH
CENTURY B.C.

fact dramatic illusions, short moments in the larger flow of events, which is fluid, dynamic, and susceptible to alteration through careful strategy. This way of thinking finds no honor or morality in wasting time, energy, and lives in battles. Instead wars of attrition are seen as lazy, reflecting the primitive human tendency to fight back reactively, without thinking.

In a society full of attrition fighters, you will gain an instant advantage by converting to maneuver. Your thought process will become more fluid, more on the side of life, and you will be able to thrive off the rigid, battle-obsessed tendencies of the people around you. By always thinking first about the overall situation and about how to maneuver people into positions of weakness rather than fight them, you will make your battles less bloody—which, since life is long and conflict is endless, is wise if you want a fruitful and enduring career. And a war of maneuver is just as decisive as a war of attrition. Think of weakening your enemies as ripening them like grain, ready to be cut down at the right moment.

The following are the four main principles of maneuver warfare:

Craft a plan with branches. Maneuver warfare depends on planning, and the plan has to be right. Too rigid and you leave yourself no room to adjust to the inevitable chaos and friction of war; too loose and unforeseen events will confuse and overwhelm you. The perfect plan stems from a detailed analysis of the situation, which allows you to decide on the best direction to follow or the perfect position to occupy and suggests several effective options (branches) to take, depending on what the enemy throws at you. A plan with branches lets you outmaneuver your enemy because your responses to changing circumstances are faster and more rational.

Give yourself room to maneuver. You cannot be mobile, you cannot maneuver freely, if you put yourself in cramped spaces or tie yourself down to positions that do not allow you to move. Consider the ability to move and keeping open more options than your enemy has as more important than holding territories or possessions. You want open space, not dead positions. This means not burdening yourself with commitments that will limit your options. It means not taking stances that leave you nowhere to go. The need for space is psychological as well as physical: you must have an unfettered mind to create anything worthwhile.

Give your enemy dilemmas, not problems. Most of your opponents are likely to be clever and resourceful; if your maneuvers simply present them with a problem, they will inevitably solve it. But a dilemma is different: whatever they do, however they respond—retreat, advance, stay still— they are still in trouble. Make every option bad: if you maneuver quickly to a point, for instance, you can force your enemies either to fight before they are ready or to retreat. Try constantly to put them in positions that seem alluring but are traps.

Create maximum disorder. Your enemy depends on being able to read you, to get some sense of your intentions. The goal of your maneuvers should be to make that impossible, to send the enemy on a wild-goose chase for meaningless information, to create ambiguity as to which way you are going to jump. The more you break down people's ability to reason about you, the more disorder you inject into their system. The disorder you create is controlled and purposeful, at least for you. The disorder the enemy suffers is debilitating and destructive.

Image:
The Sickle.
The simplest
of instruments.
To cut the tall grass
or unripened fields
of wheat with it is
exhausting labor.
But let the stalks
turn golden brown,
hard and dry, and
in that brief time
even the dullest
sickle will mow the
wheat with ease.

Authority: Battles are won by slaughter and maneuver. The greater the general, the more he contributes in maneuver, the less he demands in slaughter. . . . Nearly all the battles which are regarded as masterpieces of the military art . . . have been battles of maneuver in which very often the enemy has found himself defeated by some novel expedient or device, some queer, swift, unexpected thrust or stratagem. In such battles the losses of the victors have been small. — *Winston Churchill (1874–1965)*

21

NEGOTIATE WHILE ADVANCING THE DIPLOMATIC-WAR STRATEGY

People will always try to take from you in negotiation what they could not get from you in battle or direct confrontation. They will even use appeals to fairness and morality as a cover to advance their position. Do not be taken in: negotiation is about maneuvering for power or placement, and you must always put yourself in the kind of strong position that makes it impossible for the other side to nibble away at you during your talks. Before and during negotiations, you must keep advancing, creating relentless pressure and compelling the other side to settle on your terms. The more you take, the more you can give back in meaningless concessions. Create a reputation for being tough and uncompromising, so that people are back on their heels before they even meet you.

Therefore, a prudent ruler ought not to keep faith when by so doing it would be against his interest. . . . If men were all good, this precept would not be a good one; but as they are bad, and would not observe their faith with you, so you are not bound to keep faith with them. Nor have legitimate grounds ever failed a prince who wished to show colorable excuse for the nonfulfillment of his promise.

THE PRINCE,
NICCOLÒ
MACHIAVELLI
(1469–1527)

KEYS TO WARFARE

Conflict and confrontation are generally unpleasant affairs that churn up unpleasant emotions. Out of a desire to avoid such unpleasantness, people will often try to be nice and conciliatory to those around them, in the belief that this will elicit the same response in return. But so often experience proves this logic to be wrong: over time, the people you treat nicely will take you for granted. They will see you as weak and exploitable. Being generous does not elicit gratitude but creates either a spoiled child or someone who resents behavior perceived as charity.

Those who believe against the evidence that niceness breeds niceness in return are doomed to failure in any kind of negotiation, let alone in the game of life. People respond in a nice and conciliatory way only when it is in their interest and when they have to do so. Your goal is to create that imperative by making it painful for them to fight. If you ease up the pressure out of a desire to be conciliatory and gain their trust, you only give them an opening to procrastinate, deceive, and take advantage of your niceness. That is human nature. Over the centuries those who have fought wars have learned this lesson the hard way.

By continuing to advance, by keeping up unrelenting pressure, you force your enemies to respond and ultimately to negotiate. If you advance a little further every day, attempts to delay negotiation only make their position weaker. You are demonstrating your resolve and determination, not through symbolic gestures but by administering real pain.

You do not continue to advance in order to grab land or possessions but to put yourself in the strongest possible position and win the war. Once you have forced them to settle, you have room to make concessions and give back some of what you've taken. In the process you might even seem nice and conciliatory.

Sometimes in life you will find yourself holding the weak hand, the hand without any real leverage. At those times it is even more important to keep advancing. By demonstrating strength and resolve and maintaining the pressure, you cover up your weaknesses and gain footholds that will let you manufacture leverage for yourself.

Understand: if you are weak and ask for little, little is what you will get. But if you act strong, making firm, even outrageous demands, you will create the opposite impression: people will think that your confidence must be based on something real. You will earn respect, which in turn will translate into leverage. Once you are able to establish yourself in a stronger position, you can take this further by refusing to compromise, making it clear that you are willing to walk away from the table—an effective form of coercion. The other side may call your bluff, but you make sure there's a price to pay for this—bad publicity, for instance. And if in the end you do compromise a little, it will still be a lot less than the compromises they would have forced on you if they could.

The great British diplomat and writer Harold Nicolson believed there were two kinds of negotiators: warriors and shopkeepers. Warriors use negotiations as a way to gain time and a stronger position. Shopkeepers operate on the principle that it is more important to establish trust, to moderate each side's demands and come to a mutually satisfying settlement. Whether in diplomacy or in business, the problem arises when shopkeepers assume they are dealing with another shopkeeper only to find they are facing a warrior.

It would be helpful to know beforehand which kind of negotiator you face. The difficulty is that skillful warriors will make themselves masters of disguise: at first they will seem sincere and friendly, then will reveal their warrior nature when it is too late for you. In resolving a conflict with an enemy you do not know well, it is always best to protect yourself by playing the warrior yourself: negotiate while advancing. There will always be time to back off and fix things if you go too far. But if you fall prey to a warrior, you will be unable to recoup anything. In a world in which there are more and more warriors, you must be willing to wield the sword as well, even if you are a shopkeeper at heart.

Image: The Big Stick. You may speak softly and nicely, but the other side sees that you hold something fearsome in your hand. He does not have to feel the actual pain of it striking his head; he knows the stick is there, that it is not going away, that you have used it before, and that it hurts. Better to end the argument and negotiate a settlement, at whatever price, than risk a painful thwack.

Authority: Let us not consider ourselves victorious until the day *after* battle, nor defeated until four days later.... Let us always carry the sword in one hand and the olive branch in the other, always ready to negotiate but negotiating only while advancing.
—*Prince Klemens von Metternich (1773–1859)*

22

KNOW HOW TO END THINGS
THE EXIT STRATEGY

You are judged in this world by how well you bring things to an end. A messy or incomplete conclusion can reverberate for years to come, ruining your reputation in the process. The art of ending things well is knowing when to stop, never going so far that you exhaust yourself or create bitter enemies that embroil you in conflict in the future. It also entails ending on the right note, with energy and flair. It is not a question of simply winning the war but the way you win it, the way your victory sets you up for the next round. The height of strategic wisdom is to avoid all conflicts and entanglements from which there are no realistic exits.

KEYS TO WARFARE

If one overshoots the goal, one cannot hit it. If a bird will not come to its nest but flies higher and higher, it eventually falls into the hunter's net. He who in times of extraordinary salience of small things does not know how to call a halt, but restlessly seeks to press on and on, draws upon himself misfortune at the hands of gods and men, because he deviates from the order of nature.

THE I CHING, CHINA, CIRCA EIGHTH CENTURY B.C.

There are three kinds of people in the world. First, there are the dreamers and talkers, who begin their projects with a burst of enthusiasm. But this burst of energy quickly peters out as they encounter the real world and the hard work needed to bring any project to an end. They are emotional creatures who live mainly in the moment; they easily lose interest as something new grabs their attention. Their lives are littered with half-finished projects, including some that barely make it beyond a daydream.

Then there are those who bring whatever they do to a conclusion, either because they have to or because they can manage the effort. But they cross the finish line with distinctly less enthusiasm and energy than they had starting out. This mars the end of the campaign. Because they are impatient to finish, the ending seems hurried and patched together. And it leaves other people feeling slightly unsatisfied; it is not memorable, does not last, has no resonance.

Both of these types begin each project without a firm idea of how to end it. And as the project progresses, inevitably differing from what they had imagined it would be, they become unsure how to get out of it and either give up or simply rush to the end.

The third group comprises those who understand a primary law of power and strategy: the end of something—a project, a campaign, a conversation—has inordinate importance for people. It resonates in the mind. A war can begin with great fanfare and can bring many victories, but if it ends badly, that is all anyone remembers.

Knowing the importance and the emotional resonance of the ending of anything, people of the third type understand that the issue is not simply finishing what they have started but finishing it well—with energy, a clear head, and an eye on the afterglow, the way the event will linger in people's minds. These types invariably begin with a clear plan. When setbacks come, as setbacks will, they are able to stay patient and think rationally. They plan not just to the end but past it, to the aftermath. These are the ones who create things that last—a meaningful peace, a memorable work of art, a long and fruitful career.

Brilliant plans and piled-up conquests are not enough. You can become the victim of your own success, letting victory seduce you into going too far, creating hard-bitten enemies, winning the battle but losing the political game after it. What you need is a strategic third eye: the ability to stay focused on the future while operating in the present and ending your actions in a way that will serve your interests for the next round of war. This third eye will help you counteract the emotions that can insidiously infect your clever strategies, particularly anger and the desire for revenge.

The critical question in war is knowing when to stop, when to make your exit and come to terms. Stop too soon and you lose whatever you might have gained by advancing; you allow too little time for the conflict to show you where it is heading. Stop too late and you sacrifice your gains by exhausting yourself, grabbing more than you can handle, creating an angry and vengeful enemy.

If you concentrate exclusively on victory, with no thought for the after-effect, you may be too exhausted to profit by the peace, while it is almost certain that the peace will be a bad one, containing the germs of another war. This is a lesson supported by abundant experience.

STRATEGY, B. H. LIDDELL HART, 1954

Imagine that everything you do has a moment of perfection and fruition. Your goal is to end your project there, at such a peak. Succumb to tiredness, boredom, or impatience for the end and you fall short of that peak. Greed and delusions of grandeur will make you go too far. To conclude at this moment of perfection, you must have the clearest possible sense of your goals, of what you really want. You must also command an in-depth knowledge of your resources— how far can you practicably go? This kind of awareness will give you an intuitive feel for the culminating point.

Victory and defeat are what you make of them; it is how you deal with them that matters. Since defeat is inevitable in life, you must master the art of losing well and strategically. First, think of your own mental outlook, how you absorb defeat psychologically. See it as a temporary setback, something to wake you up and teach you a lesson, and even as you lose, you end on a high note and with an edge: you are mentally prepared to go on the offensive in the next round. So often, those who have success become soft and imprudent; you must welcome defeat as a way to make yourself stronger.

Second, you must see any defeat as a way to demonstrate something positive about yourself and your character to other people. This means standing tall, not showing signs of bitterness or becoming defensive.

Third, if you see that defeat is inevitable, it is often best to go down swinging. That way you end on a high note even as you lose. This helps to rally the troops, giving them hope for the future. Planting the seeds of future victory in present defeat is strategic brilliance of the highest order.

Finally, since any ending is a kind of beginning of the next phase, it is often wise strategy to end on an ambivalent note. If you are reconciling with an enemy after a fight, subtly hint that you still have a residue of doubt—that the other side must still prove itself to you. When a campaign or project comes to an end, leave people feeling that they cannot foresee what you will do next—keep them in suspense, toying with their attention. By ending on a note of mystery and ambiguity—a mixed signal, an insinuating comment, a touch of doubt—you gain the upper hand for the next round in a most subtle and insidious fashion.

Image:
The Sun. When it
finishes its course and
sets below the horizon, it
leaves behind a brilliant
and memorable after-
glow. Its return is
always desired.

Authority: To conquer is nothing. One must profit from one's success. —*Napoleon Bonaparte (1769–1821)*

UNCONVENTIONAL (DIRTY) WARFARE

A general fighting a war must constantly search for an advantage over the opponent. The greatest advantage comes from the element of surprise, from hitting enemies with strategies that are novel, outside their experience, completely unconventional. It is in the nature of war, however, that over time any strategy with any possible application will be tried and tested, so that the search for the new and unconventional has an innate tendency to become more and more extreme. At the same time, moral and ethical codes that governed warfare for centuries have gradually loosened. These two effects dovetail into what we today call "dirty war," where anything goes, down to the killing of thousands of unwarned civilians. Dirty war is political, deceptive, and supremely manipulative. Often the last recourse of the weak and desperate, it uses any means available to level the playing field.

The unconventional has its own logic that you must understand. First, nothing stays new for long. Those who depend on novelty must constantly come up with some fresh idea that goes against the orthodoxies of the time. Second, people who use unconventional methods are very hard to fight. The classic, direct route—the use of force and strength—does not work. You must use indirect methods to combat indirection, fight fire with fire, even at the cost of going dirty yourself. To try to stay clean out of a sense of morality is to risk defeat.

The chapters in this section will initiate you into the various forms of the unorthodox. They are designed to give you a greater understanding of the diabolical psychology involved in each strategy, helping to arm you with the proper defense.

23

WEAVE A SEAMLESS BLEND OF FACT AND FICTION MISPERCEPTION STRATEGIES

Since no creature can survive without the ability to see or sense what is going on around it, you must make it hard for your enemies to know what is going on around them, *including what you are doing. Disturb their focus and you weaken their strategic powers. People's perceptions are filtered through their emotions; they tend to interpret the world according to what they want to see. Feed their expectations, manufacture a reality to match their desires, and they will fool themselves. The best deceptions are based on ambiguity, mixing fact and fiction so that the one cannot be disentangled from the other. Control people's perceptions of reality and you control them.*

KEYS TO WARFARE

In the early history of warfare, military leaders were faced with the following predicament: The success of any war effort depended on the ability to know as much about the other side—its intentions, its strengths and weaknesses—as possible. But the enemy would never willingly disclose this information.

The only solution was to scrutinize the enemy for outward signs of what was going on within. A strategist might count the cooking fires in the enemy camp, for example, and the changes in that number over time; that would show the army's size and whether it was increasing as reserves arrived or decreasing as it was split, or perhaps as soldiers deserted.

The leader also knew that just as he was watching the other side, the other side was doing the same with him. In pondering this back-and-forth game of reading appearances, certain enlightened strategists in cultures around the world had a similar epiphany: Why not deliberately distort the signs the enemy was looking at? Why not mislead by playing with appearances? If the enemy is counting our cooking fires, just as we are counting theirs, why not light more fires, or fewer, to create a false impression of our strength? An enemy that thinks it knows our size and intentions, and is unaware that it has been misled, will act on its false knowledge and commit all kinds of mistakes. It will move its men to fight an enemy that is not there. It will fight with shadows.

We face a similar dynamic in our daily battles in life. We are social creatures, and our happiness, even our survival, depends on our ability to understand what other people are intending and thinking. But because we cannot get inside their heads, we are forced to read the signs in their outward behavior. That is why, in the social realm, we learn from an early age to use deception—we tell others what they want to hear, concealing our real thoughts, hedging with the truth, misleading to make a better impression. Many of these deceptions are entirely unconscious.

Since appearances are critical and deception is inevitable, what you want is to elevate your game—to make your deceptions more conscious and skillful. There is a lot you can learn from the military arts of deception, which are based on timeless laws of psychology and are infinitely applicable to the battles of daily life.

The following are the six main forms of military deception, each with its own advantage.

The false front. This is the oldest form of military deception. It originally involved making the enemy believe that one was weaker than in fact was the case. A leader would feign a retreat, say, baiting a trap for the enemy to rush into, luring it into an ambush.

Controlling the front you present to the world is the most critical deceptive skill. People respond most directly to what they see, to what is most visible to their eyes. If you seem clever—if you seem deceptive—their guard will be up and it will be impossible to mislead them. Instead you need to present a front that does the opposite—disarms suspicions. The best front here is weakness, which will make the other side feel superior to you.

Betrayer's masterpiece.—
To express to a fellow conspirator the grievous suspicion that one is going to be betrayed by him, and to do so at precisely the moment one is oneself engaged in betrayal, is a masterpiece of malice, because it keeps the other occupied with himself and compels him for a time to behave very openly and unsuspiciously, thus giving the actual betrayer full freedom of action.

HUMAN, ALL TOO HUMAN, FRIEDRICH NIETZSCHE, 1878

In general you should present a face to the world that promises the opposite of what you are actually planning. If you are getting ready to attack, seem unprepared for a fight or too comfortable and relaxed to be plotting war.

The decoy attack. This is another ruse dating back to ancient times, and it remains perhaps the military's most common deceptive ploy. It began as a solution to a problem: if the enemy knew you were going to attack point A, they would put all their defenses there and make your job too difficult. The only answer was to march your army toward point B or, better, to send part of your army in that direction while holding troops in reserve for your real objective.

The decoy attack is also a critical strategy in daily life, where you must retain the power to hide your intentions. To keep people from defending the points you want to attack, you must follow the military model and make real gestures toward a goal that does not interest you.

Camouflage. The ability to blend into the environment is one of the most terrifying forms of military deception. Preventing your enemies from seeing you until it is too late is a devastating way to control their perceptions.

The camouflage strategy can be applied to daily life in two ways. First, it is always good to be able to blend into the social landscape, to avoid calling attention to yourself unless you choose to do so. Second, if you are preparing an attack of some sort and begin by blending into the environment, showing no sign of activity, your attack will seem to come out of nowhere, doubling its power.

The hypnotic pattern: Human beings naturally tend to think in terms of patterns. They like to see events conforming to their expectations by fitting into a pattern or scheme, for schemes, whatever their actual content, comfort us by suggesting that the chaos of life is predictable. This mental habit offers excellent ground for deception—deliberately creating some pattern to make your enemies believe that your next action will follow true to form. Having lulled them into complacency, you now have room to work against their expectations, break the pattern, and take them by surprise.

Planted information. People are much more likely to believe something they see with their own eyes than something they are told. They are more likely to believe something they discover than something pushed at them.

No matter how good a liar you are, when you deceive, it is hard to be completely natural. That is why it is so effective to spread your deceptions through people whom you keep ignorant of the truth—people who believe the lie themselves. When working with double agents of this kind, it is always wise to initially feed them some true information—this will establish the credibility of the intelligence they pass along. After that they will be the perfect conduits for your lies.

Shadows within shadows. Deceptive maneuvers are like shadows deliberately

In war-time, truth is so precious that she should always be attended by a bodyguard of lies.

WINSTON CHURCHILL, 1874–1965

cast: the enemy responds to them as if they were solid and real, which in and of itself is a mistake. In a sophisticated, competitive world, however, both sides know the game, and the alert enemy will not necessarily grasp at the shadow you have thrown. So you have to take the art of deception to a level higher, casting shadows *within* shadows, making it impossible for your enemies to distinguish between fact and fiction. You make everything so ambiguous and uncertain, spread so much fog, that even if you are suspected of deceit, it does not matter—the truth cannot be unraveled from the lies, and all their suspicion gives them is torment. Meanwhile, as they strain to figure out what you are up to, they waste valuable time and resources.

Image:
Fog. It makes the
shape and color of objects
impossible to know. Learn to
create enough of it and you
free yourself of the enemy's
intrusive gaze; you have room to
maneuver. You know where you are
headed, while the enemy
goes astray, deeper
and deeper into
the fog.

Authority: One who is good at combating the enemy fools it with inscrutable moves, confuses it with false intelligence, makes it relax by concealing one's strength, . . . deafens its ears by jumbling one's orders and signals, blinds its eyes by converting one's banners and insignias, . . . confounds its battle plan by providing distorted facts. — *Tou Bi Fu Tan, A Scholar's Dilettante Remarks on War (16th century* A.D.*)*

24

TAKE THE LINE OF LEAST EXPECTATION THE ORDINARY-EXTRAORDINARY STRATEGY

People expect your behavior to conform to known patterns and conventions. Your task as a strategist is to upset their expectations. Surprise them and chaos and unpredictability—which they try desperately to keep at bay—enter their world, and in the ensuing mental disturbance, their defenses are down and they are vulnerable. First, do something ordinary and conventional to fix their image of you, then hit them with the extraordinary. The terror is greater for being so sudden. Never rely on an unorthodox strategy that worked before—it is conventional the second time around. Sometimes the ordinary is extraordinary because it is unexpected.

UNCONVENTIONAL WARFARE

Thousands of years ago, military leaders—aware of the incredibly high stakes involved in war—would search high and low for anything that could bring their army an advantage on the battlefield. Some generals who were particularly clever would devise novel troop formations or an innovative use of infantry or cavalry: the newness of the tactic would prevent the enemy from anticipating it. Being unexpected, it would create confusion in the enemy. An army that gained the advantage of surprise in this way could often leverage it into victory on the battlefield and perhaps a string of victories.

The enemy, however, would work hard to come up with a defense against the new strategy, whatever it was, and would often find one quite fast. So what once brought brilliant success and was the epitome of innovation soon no longer worked and in fact became conventional. Furthermore, in the process of working out a defense against a novel strategy, the enemy itself would often be forced to innovate; now it was their turn to introduce something surprising and horribly effective. And so the cycle would go on. War has always been ruthless; nothing stays unconventional for long. It is either innovate or die.

In modern times the constant challenge to top the enemy with something new and unconventional has taken a turn into dirty warfare. Loosening the codes of honor and morality that in the past limited what a general could do (at least to some extent), modern armies have slowly embraced the idea that anything goes. Guerrilla and terrorist tactics have been known since ancient times; now they have become not only more common but more strategic and refined. Propaganda, disinformation, psychological warfare, deception, and political means of waging war have all become active ingredients in any unconventional strategy. A counterstrategy usually develops to deal with the latest in dirty warfare, but it often involves falling to the enemy's level, fighting fire with fire. The dirty enemy adapts by sinking to a dirtier level still, creating a downward spiral.

This dynamic is particularly intense in warfare but it permeates every aspect of human activity. If you are in politics and business and your opponents or competitors come up with a novel strategy, you must adapt it for your own purposes or, better, top it. Their once new tactic becomes conventional and ultimately useless. Our world is so fiercely competitive that one side will almost always end up resorting to something dirty, something outside earlier codes of accepted behavior. Ignore this spiral out of a sense of morality or pride and you put yourself at a severe disadvantage; you are called to respond—in all likelihood to fight a little dirty yourself.

The spiral dominates not just politics or business but culture as well, with its desperate search for the shocking and novel to gain attention and win momentary acclaim. Anything goes. The speed of the process has grown exponentially with time; what was unconventional in the arts a few years ago now seems unbearably trite and the height of conformity.

What we consider unconventional has

Make a false move, not to pass it for a genuine one but to transform it into a genuine one after the enemy has been convinced of its falsity.

THE WILES OF WAR: 36 MILITARY STRATEGIES FROM ANCIENT CHINA, TRANSLATED BY SUN HAICHEN, 1991 changed over the years, but the laws that make unconventionality effective, being based on elemental psychology, are timeless. And once you understand the essence of unconventional warfare, you will be able to use it in your daily life.

Unconventional warfare has four main principles, as gleaned from the great practitioners of the art.

Work outside the enemy's experience. Principles of war are based on precedent: a kind of canon of strategies and counterstrategies develops over the centuries, and since war is so dangerously chaotic, strategists come to rely on these principles for lack of anything else. They filter what's happening now through what happened in the past. The armies that have shaken the world, though, have always found a way to operate outside the canon, and thus outside the enemy's experience. This ability imposes chaos and disorder on the enemy, which cannot orient itself to novelty and collapses in the process.

Your task as a strategist is to know your enemies well, then use your knowledge to contrive a strategy that goes outside their experience. What they might have read or heard about matters less than their personal experience, which dominates their emotional lives and determines their responses. Once a strategy is used and is no longer outside your enemy's experience, though, it will not have the same effect if repeated.

Unfold the extraordinary out of the ordinary. To the ancient Chinese, doing something extraordinary had little effect without a setup of something ordinary. You had to mix the two—to fix your opponents' expectations with some banal, ordinary maneuver, a comfortable pattern that they would then expect you to follow. With the enemy sufficiently mesmerized, you would then hit it with the extraordinary, a show of stunning force from an entirely new angle. Framed by the predictable, the blow would have double the impact.

The unconventional maneuver that confused enemies, though, would have become conventional the second or third time around. So the wily general might then go back to the ordinary strategy that he had used earlier to fix their attention and use it for his main attack, for that would be the last thing the enemy would expect. And so the ordinary and the extraordinary are effective only if they play off each other in a constant spiraling manner. This applies to culture as much as to war: to gain attention with some cultural product, you have to create something new, but something with no reference to ordinary life is not in fact unconventional, but merely strange. What is truly shocking and extraordinary unfolds out of the ordinary. The intertwining of the ordinary and extraordinary is the very definition of surrealism.

Act crazy like a fox. Despite appearances, a lot of disorder and irrationality lurks beneath the surface of society and individuals. That is why we so desperately strain to maintain order and why people acting irrationally can be terrifying: they are demonstrating that they have lost the walls we build to keep out the irrational. We cannot predict what they will do next, and we tend to give them a wide berth—it is not worth mixing it up with such sources of chaos. On the other hand, these people can also inspire a kind of awe and respect, for secretly we all desire access to the irrational seas churning inside us. In ancient times the insane were seen as divinely possessed; a residue of that attitude survives. The greatest generals have all had a touch of divine, strategic madness.

The secret is to keep this streak under control. Upon occasion you allow yourself to operate in a way that is deliberately irrational, but less is more—do this too much and you may be locked up. You will in any case frighten people more by showing an occasional flash of insanity, just enough to keep everyone off balance and wondering what will come next. As an alternative, act somewhat randomly, as if what you did were determined by a roll of the dice. Randomness is thoroughly disturbing to humans. Think of this behavior as a kind of therapy—a chance to indulge occasionally in the irrational, as a relief from the oppressive need to always seem normal.

Keep the wheels in constant motion. The unconventional is generally the province of the young, who are not comfortable with conventions and take great pleasure in flouting them. The danger is that as we age, we need more comfort and predictability and lose our taste for the unorthodox. You must fight the psychological aging process even more than the physical one, for a mind full of stratagems, tricks, and fluid maneuvers will keep you young. Make a point of breaking the habits you have developed, of acting in a way that is contrary to how you have operated in the past; practice a kind of unconventional warfare on your own mind. Keep the wheels turning and churning the soil so that nothing settles and clumps into the conventional.

Image:
The Plow.
The ground
must be prepared.
The blades of the plow
churn the earth in constant
motion, bringing air into the
soil. The process must go on every
year, or the most pernicious weeds will
take over and the clumped soil will choke
off all life. From the earth, plowed and fertilized,
the most nourishing and wondrous plants can emerge.

Authority: In general, in battle one engages the enemy with the orthodox and gains victory through the unorthodox. . . . The unorthodox and the orthodox mutually produce each other, just like an endless cycle. Who can exhaust them? —*Sun-tzu (fourth century B.C.)*

25

OCCUPY THE MORAL
HIGH GROUND
THE RIGHTEOUS STRATEGY

In a political world, the cause you are fighting for must seem more just than the enemy's. Think of this as moral terrain that you and the other side are fighting over; by questioning your enemies' motives and making them appear evil, you can narrow their base of support and room to maneuver. Aim at the soft spots in their public image, exposing any hypocrisies on their part. Never assume that the justice of your cause is self-evident; publicize and promote it. When you yourself come under moral attack from a clever enemy, do not whine or get angry; fight fire with fire. If possible, position yourself as the underdog, the victim, the martyr. Learn to inflict guilt as a moral weapon.

KEYS TO WARFARE

In almost all cultures, morality—the definition of good and evil— originated as a way to differentiate one class of people from another. Societies use ideas about what is and is not moral to create values that serve them well. When these values fall behind the times or otherwise cease to fit, morality slowly shifts and evolves.

There are individuals and groups, however, who use morality for a much different purpose—not to maintain social order but to extract an advantage in a competitive situation, such as war, politics or business. They are masters at occupying the high ground and translating it into some kind of power or advantage.

When your enemies try to present themselves as more justified than you are, and therefore more moral, you must see this move for what it most often is: not a reflection of morality, of right and wrong, but a clever strategy.

The only effective response is to be strategic, too. Once the fight for moral terrain has begun, you must fight to occupy the high ground in the same way you would in a shooting war.

Like any form of warfare, moral conflict has both offensive and defensive possibilities. When you are on the offense, you are actively working to destroy the enemy's reputation.

Revealing your opponent's hypocrisies is perhaps the most lethal offensive weapon in the moral arsenal: people naturally hate hypocrites. Enemies who trumpet certain values as inherent to their side yet who do not always adhere to those values in reality make juicy targets.

THE MIND OF WAR: JOHN BOYD AND AMERICAN SECURITY, GRANT T. HAMMOND, 2001

If a fight with your enemies is inevitable, always work to make them start it. Similarly, even if you are fighting a war of aggression, find a way to present yourself not as a conqueror but as a liberator. You are fighting not for land or money but to free people suffering under an oppressive regime.

In general, in a conflict that is potentially nasty, in which you are certain the enemy will resort to almost anything, it is best that you go on the offensive with your moral campaign and not wait for their attacks. Poking holes in the other side's reputation is easier than defending your own.

The best defense against moral warriors is to give them no target. Live up to your good name; practice what you preach, at least in public; ally yourself with the most just causes of the day. Make your opponents work so hard to undermine your reputation that they seem desperate, and their attacks blow up in their faces. The best defense against a moral attack is to have inoculated yourself against it beforehand, by recognizing where you may be vulnerable and taking preventive measures.

Wars are most often fought out of self-interest: a nation goes to war to protect itself against an invading, or potentially dangerous, enemy or to seize a neighbor's land or resources. Morality is sometimes a component in the decision—in a holy war or crusade, for example—but even here self-interest usually plays a role; morality is often just a cover for the desire for more territory, more riches, more power.

It is a world not of angels but of angles, where men speak of moral principles but act on power principles; a world where we are always moral and our enemies always immoral.

RULES FOR RADICALS, SAUL D. ALINSKY, 1909–1972

Successful wickedness hath obtained the name virtue ... when it is for the getting of the kingdom.

THOMAS HOBBES, 1588–1679

Wars of self-interest usually end when the winner's interests are satisfied.

Those people who fight out of a moral sense can sometimes be the most dangerous. They may be hungry for power and are using morality as a cover; they may be motivated by some dark and hidden grievance; but in any case they are after more than self-interest. Even if you beat them, or at least defend yourself against them successfully, discretion here may be the better part of valor. Avoid wars of morality if you can; they are not worth the time and dirty feelings they churn up.

Image: Germs. Once they get inside and attack the body, they spread quickly. Your attempts to destroy them often make them stronger and harder to root out. The best defense is prevention. Anticipate the attack and inoculate yourself against it. With such organisms you have to fight fire with fire.

Authority: The pivot of war is nothing but name and righteousness. Secure a good name for yourself and give the enemy a bad name; proclaim your righteousness and reveal the unrighteousness of the enemy. Then your army can set forth in a great momentum, shaking heaven and earth. — *Tou Bi Fu Tan, A Scholar's Dilettante Remarks on War (sixteenth century A.D.)*

26

DENY THEM TARGETS
THE STRATEGY OF THE VOID

The feeling of emptiness or void—silence, isolation, non-engagement with others—is for most people intolerable. As a human weakness, that fear offers fertile ground for a powerful strategy: give your enemies no target to attack, be dangerous but elusive and invisible, then watch as they chase you into the void. This is the essence of guerrilla warfare. Instead of frontal battles, deliver irritating but damaging side attacks and pinprick bites. Frustrated at their inability to use their strength against your vaporous campaign, your opponents will grow irrational and exhausted. Make your guerrilla war part of a grand political cause—a people's war—that crests in an irresistible revolution.

Such was the
system Spain
used against us.
One hundred
and fifty to two
hundred guerrilla
bands scattered
all over Spain
had sworn to
kill thirty or
forty Frenchmen
a month each:
that made six to
eight thousand
men a month
for all guerrilla
bands together.
The order was
never to attack
soldiers traveling
as a body, unless
the guerrillas
outnumbered
them. But
they fired on
all stragglers,
attacked small
escorts, and
sought to lay
hands on the
enemy's funds,
couriers, and
especially
convoys. As all
the inhabitants
acted as spies
for their fellow
citizens, the
guerrillas
knew when the
convoys would
leave and how
strong their

KEYS TO WARFARE

Over the centuries organized war has always tended to follow a certain logic, which is so universal as almost to seem inherent to the process. The logic is as follows: A leader decides to take his country to war and raises an army for that purpose. That army's goal is to meet and defeat the enemy in a decisive battle that will force a surrender and favorable peace terms. The strategist guiding the campaign must deal with a specific area, the theater of war. This area is most often relatively limited; maneuvering in vast open spaces complicates the possibility of bringing the war to closure. Working within the theater of war, then, the strategist contrives to bring his army to the decisive battle in a way that will surprise the enemy or put it at a disadvantage. To keep his forces strong enough to deliver a mortal blow, he concentrates them rather than dispersing them. It may take several battles to end the war, as each side works to dominate the key positions that will give it control of the theater, but military leaders must try to end it as quickly as possible. The longer it drags on, the more the army's resources are stretched to a breaking point where the ability to fight collapses. Soldiers' morale declines with time as well.

As with any human activity, however, this positive, orderly side generates a negative, shadow side that contains its own form of power and reverse logic. The shadow side is guerrilla warfare. The rudiments of guerrilla warfare originated thousands of years ago, when smaller nations found themselves invaded by more powerful neighbors; to survive, their armies were forced to flee the invader, for any direct engagement would have destroyed them.

The early guerrilla warriors learned the value of operating in small, dispersed bands as opposed to a concentrated army, keeping in constant motion, never forming a front, flank, or rear for the other side to hit. The enemy would want to keep the war confined to a particular space; better, then, to extend it over as much territory as possible, melting into the countryside, forcing the enemy to disperse itself in the chase, opening itself up to raids and pinprick attacks. The enemy would naturally want a quick end to the war, so it was desirable to drag it out as long as possible, making time an offensive weapon that consumed the enemy with friction and sagging morale.

The power of guerrilla warfare is essentially psychological. In conventional warfare everything converges on the engagement of two armies in battle. That is what all strategy is devised for and what the martial instinct requires as a kind of release from tension. By postponing this natural convergence indefinitely, the guerrilla strategist creates intense frustration. The longer this mental corrosion continues, the more debilitating it gets.

Because it is so psychological, guerrilla strategy is infinitely applicable to social conflict. In life as in war, our thoughts and emotions naturally converge on moments of contact and engagement with others. We find people who are deliberately elusive, who evade contact, extremely disconcerting. These opponents can gain a disturbing power over our minds, and the longer they

escorts would be, and the bands would make sure they were twice the size. They knew the country very well, and they would attack furiously in the most favorable spot. Success often crowned the undertaking; but they always killed a lot of men, and the goal was achieved. As there are twelve months in the year, we were losing about eighty thousand men a year, without any pitched battles. The war in Spain lasted seven years, so over five hundred men were killed.... But that includes only those killed by the guerrillas. Add the battles of Salamanca, Talavera, and Vitoria, and several others that our troops lost; the sieges,... the fruitless attack on Cádiz; add *too the invasion and evacuation of Portugal, the fevers and various illnesses that the temperature caused our soldiers to suffer, and you will see that we could add a further three hundred thousand men to that number during those seven years. . . . . . . From what has been said, it will be apparent that the prime aim of this sort of war is to bring about the destruction of the enemy almost without him noticing it, and as a drop of water dripping on a stone will eventually dig a hole in the stone, patience and perseverance are needed, always following the same system. In the long run, the enemy will suffer more from this than he would*

keep it up, the more we are sucked into fighting on their terms.

The primary consideration should always be whether a guerrilla-style campaign is appropriate for the circumstances you are facing. It is especially effective, for instance, against an opponent who is aggressive yet clever. These types cannot stand lack of contact with an enemy. They live to maneuver, outwit, and outhit. Having nothing to strike at neutralizes their cleverness, and their aggression becomes their downfall.

Once you have determined that a guerrilla war is appropriate, take a look at the army you will use. A large, conventional army is never suitable; fluidity and the ability to strike from many angles are what counts. The organizational model is the cell—a relatively small group of men and women, tight-knit, dedicated, self-motivated, and spread out. These cells should penetrate the enemy camp itself.

The main point is to avoid an organization's formal channels and tendency for bigness and concentration. Opt for mobility instead; make your army light and clandestine. You can also attach your guerrilla cells to a regular army. This mix of conventional and unconventional can prove highly effective.

Once you have organized your cells, you must find a way to lure the enemy into attacking you. In war this is generally accomplished by retreating, then turning to strike at the enemy with constant small raids and ambushes that cannot be ignored.

In most conflicts time is a danger, bringing Murphy's Law into play: if anything can go wrong, it will. If your army is small and relatively self-sufficient, though, there is less to go wrong, and meanwhile you are working to make sure that for the enemy the passage of time is a nightmare. Morale is sinking, resources are stretched. The effect is exponential: as unexpected problems crop up, the enemy starts making mistakes.

Make time an offensive weapon in your strategizing. Design your maneuvers to keep your enemies just barely going, always thinking that one more battle will do the trick. You want them to deteriorate slowly; a sudden sharp setback, a clear view of the trap you are laying for them, and they will pull out before the damage is done. Let them take key positions that give them the illusion of success. They will hold on to them tenaciously as your raids and pinprick attacks grow in number. Then, as they weaken, increase the pace of these attacks. Let them hope, let them think it is all still worth it, until the trap is set. Then break their illusion.

The essence of guerrilla warfare is fluidity. The enemy will always try to adjust to what you are doing, attempting to find its feet in this unfamiliar terrain. You must be prepared to change and adopt whatever is contrary to expectation: this might mean occasionally fighting in a conventional manner, concentrating your army to attack here or there, then dispersing again. Your goal is maximum disorder and unfamiliarity. Remember: this war is psychological. It is the enemies' minds that are grasping at air and their minds that fall first.

from losing pitched battles.

ON PARTISANS AND IRREGULAR FORCES, J.F.A. LE MIÈRE DE CORVEY, 1823

Image: The Mosquito. Most animals present a front, back, and sides that can be attacked or threatened. Mosquitoes, though, give you nothing but an irritating whir in the ear, from all sides and angles. You cannot hit them, you cannot see them. Your flesh, meanwhile, affords them endless targets. Enough bites and you realize that the only solution is to stop fighting and move as far away as possible.

Authority: Anything that has form can be overcome; anything that takes shape can be countered. This is why sages conceal their forms in nothingness and let their minds soar in the void.
—*Huainanzi (second century B.C.)*

27

SEEM TO WORK FOR THE INTERESTS OF OTHERS WHILE FURTHERING YOUR OWN
THE ALLIANCE STRATEGY

The best way to advance your cause with the minimum of effort and bloodshed is to create a constantly shifting network of alliances, getting others to compensate for your deficiencies, do your dirty work, fight your wars, spend energy pulling you forward. The art is in choosing those allies who fit the needs of the moment and fill the gaps in your power. Give them gifts, offer them friendship, help them in time of need—all to blind them to reality and put them under subtle obligation to you. At the same time, work to sow dissension in the alliances of others, weakening your enemies by isolating them. While forming convenient coalitions, keep yourself free of negative entanglements.

Six in the third place means: He finds a comrade. Now he beats the drum, now he stops. Now he sobs, now he sings. Here the source of a man's strength lies not in himself but in his relation to other people. No matter how close to them he may be, if his center of gravity depends on them, he is inevitably tossed to and fro between joy and sorrow. Rejoicing to high heaven, then sad unto death—this is the fate of those who depend upon an inner accord with other persons whom they love. . . .

THE I CHING, CHINA, CIRCA EIGHTH CENTURY B.C.

KEYS TO WARFARE

To survive and advance at all in life, we find ourselves constantly having to use other people for some purpose, some need—to obtain resources we cannot get on our own, to give us protection of some sort, to compensate for a skill or talent we do not possess. As a description of human relationships, however, the word "use" has ugly connotations, and in any case we always like to make our actions seem nobler than they are. We prefer to think of these interactions as relationships of assistance, partnering, friendship.

The first step is to understand that all of us constantly use other people to help and advance ourselves. There is no shame in this, no need to ever feel guilty. Nor should we take it personally when we realize that someone else is using us; using people is a human and social necessity. Next, with this understanding in mind, you must learn to make these necessary alliances strategic ones, aligning yourself with people who can give you something you cannot get on your own. The alliances that will help you most are those involving mutual self-interest.

Think of your alliances as stepping-stones toward a goal. Over the course of your life, you will be constantly jumping from one stone to the next to suit your needs. When this particular river is crossed, you will leave them behind you.

You must be realistic to the core, thinking far ahead and keeping the situation as fluid as possible. The ally of today may be the enemy of tomorrow. Sentiment has no place in the picture. If you are weak but clever, you can slowly leapfrog into a position of strength by bouncing from one alliance to another. The opposite approach is to make a key alliance and stick with it, valuing trust and an established relationship. This can work well in stable times, but in periods of flux, which are more common, it can prove to be your undoing: differences in interest will inevitably emerge, and at the same time it will become hard to disentangle yourself from a relationship in which so much emotion has been invested. It is safer to bank on change, to keep your options open and your alliances based on need, not loyalty or shared values.

The key to playing the game is to recognize who can best advance your interests at that moment. This need not be the most obviously powerful person on the scene, the person who *seems* to be able to do most for you; alliances that meet specific needs or answer particular deficiencies are often more useful. (Grand alliances between two great powers are generally the least effective.)

It is a common strategy in bicycle races not to go out in front but to stay right behind the leader, a position that cuts down wind resistance—the leader faces the wind for you and saves you energy. At the last minute, you sprint ahead. Letting other people cut resistance for you and waste their energy on your behalf is the height of economy and strategy.

One of the best stratagems is to begin by seeming to help another person in some cause or fight, only for the purpose of furthering your own interests in the end. It is easy to find such people: they have a glaring need, a temporary weakness that you can help them to overcome. Now you have put them

I regarded most of the people I met solely and exclusively as creatures I could use as porters in my voyages of ambition. Almost all these porters sooner or later became exhausted. Unable to endure the long marches that I forced on them at top speed and under all climatic conditions, they died on the way. I took others. To attach them to my service, I promised to get them to where I myself was going to that endstation of glory which climbers desperately want to reach....

THE SECRET LIFE OF SALVADOR DALÍ, SALVADOR DALÍ, 1942

A lion and a wild ass entered into an agreement to hunt wild beasts together. The lion was to use his great strength, while the ass would make use of his greater speed. When they had taken a certain number of animals, the lion divided up the spoils into three portions. "I'll take the first share because I am the king," he said. "The second share will be mine because I have been your partner in the chase," he said. "As for the third share," he said to the wild ass, "this share will be a great source of harm to you, believe me, if you do not yield it up to me. And, by the way, get lost!" It is suitable always to calculate your own strength,

under a subtle obligation to you, to use as you will—to dominate their affairs, to divert their energies in the direction you desire. The emotions you create with your offer of help will blind the other person to your ulterior purpose.

A variation is to play the mediator, the center around which other powers pivot. While remaining covertly autonomous, you make those around you fight for your allegiance. The brilliance of this variation is that merely by assuming a central position, you can wield tremendous power. You can maintain power in this central position only by keeping yourself unentangled and courted by all. The moment you enter into any kind of lasting alliance, your power is greatly reduced.

A key component is the ability to manipulate other people's alliances and even destroy them, sowing dissension among your opponents so that they fight among themselves. Breaking your enemy's alliances is as good as making alliances yourself.

Your focus here is on stirring up mistrust. Make one partner suspicious of the other, spread rumors, cast doubts on people's motives, be friendly to one ally to make the other jealous. Divide and conquer. People will accuse you of being feckless, amoral, treacherous. Do not let them get to you. The only real danger is that your reputation will eventually keep people from making alliances with you—but self-interest rules the world. If you are seen to have benefited others in the past and as capable of doing the same in the present, you will have suitors and playing partners. Besides, you are loyal and generous, as long as there is mutual need. And when you show that you cannot be had by the false lure of permanent loyalty and friendship, you will actually find yourself treated with greater respect. Many will be drawn to your realistic and spirited way of playing the game.

and not to enter into an alliance with people stronger than yourself.

FABLES, AESOP, SIXTH CENTURY B.C.

Image: Stepping-stones. The stream runs fast and dangerous, but you must cross it at some point. There lie some stones in a haphazard line that can get you to the other side. If you linger too long on one stone, you will lose your balance. If you go too fast or skip one, you will slip. Instead you must jump lightly from one stone to the next and never look back.

Authority: Beware of sentimental alliances where the consciousness of good deeds is the only compensation for noble sacrifices. —*Otto von Bismarck (1815–1898)*

28

GIVE YOUR RIVALS ENOUGH ROPE TO HANG THEMSELVES THE ONE-UPMANSHIP STRATEGY

Life's greatest dangers often come not from external enemies but from our supposed colleagues and friends, who pretend to work for the common cause while scheming to sabotage us and steal our ideas for their gain. Although, in the court in which you serve, you must maintain the appearance of consideration and civility, you also must learn to defeat these people. Work to instill doubts and insecurities in such rivals, getting them to think too much and act defensively. Bait them with subtle challenges that get under their skin, triggering an overreaction, an embarrassing mistake. The victory you are after is to isolate them. Make them hang themselves through their own self-destructive tendencies, leaving you blameless and clean.

*In my own view
(but compare
Motherwell)
there is only one
correct time when
the gamesman
can give advice:
and that is when
the gamesman
has achieved a
useful though
not necessarily a
winning lead. Say
three up and nine
to play at golf,
or, in billiards,
sixty-five to his
opponent's thirty.
Most of the
accepted methods
are effective. E.g.
in billiards, the
old phrase serves.
It runs like this:
Gamesman:
Look . . . may I
say something?
Layman: What?
Gamesman:
Take it easy.
Layman: What
do you mean?
Gamesman: I
mean—you know
how to make
the strokes, but
you're stretching
yourself on the
rack all the time.
Look. Walk up*

THE ART OF ONE-UPMANSHIP

Throughout your life you will find yourself fighting on two fronts. First is the external front, your inevitable enemies—but second and less obvious is the internal front, your colleagues and fellow courtiers, many of whom will scheme against you, advancing their own agendas at your expense. The worst of it is that you will often have to fight on both fronts at once, facing your external enemies while also working to secure your internal position, an exhausting and debilitating struggle.

The solution is not to ignore the internal problem (you will have a short life if you do so) or to deal with it in a direct and conventional manner, by complaining, acting aggressively, or forming defensive alliances. Understand: internal warfare is by nature unconventional. Since people theoretically on the same side usually do their best to maintain the appearance of being team players working for the greater good, complaining about them or attacking them will only make you look bad and isolate you. Yet at the same time, you can expect these ambitious types to operate underhandedly and indirectly. Outwardly charming and cooperative, behind the scenes they are manipulative and slippery.

You need to adopt a form of warfare suited to these nebulous yet dangerous battles, which go on every day. And the unconventional strategy that works best in this arena is the art of one-upmanship. Developed by history's savviest courtiers, it is based on two simple premises: first, your rivals harbor the seeds of their own self-destruction, and second, a rival who is made to feel defensive and inferior, however subtly, will tend to act defensive and inferior, to his or her detriment.

People's personalities often form around weaknesses, character flaws, uncontrollable emotions. People who feel needy, or who have a superiority complex, or are afraid of chaos, or desperately want order, will develop a personality—a social mask—to cover up their flaws and make it possible for them to present a confident, pleasant, responsible exterior to the world. But the mask is like the scar tissue covering a wound: touch it the wrong way and it hurts. Your victims' responses start to go out of control: they complain, act defensive and paranoid, or show the arrogance they try so hard to conceal. For a moment the mask falls.

When you sense you have colleagues who may prove dangerous—or are actually already plotting something—you must try first to gather intelligence on them. Look at their everyday behavior, their past actions, their mistakes, for signs of their flaws. With this knowledge in hand, you are ready for the game of one-upmanship.

Begin by doing something to prick the underlying wound, creating doubt, insecurity, and anxiety. It might be an offhand comment or something that your victims sense as a challenge to their position within the court. Your goal is not to challenge them blatantly, though, but to get under their skin: they feel attacked but are not sure why or how. The result is a vague, troubling sensation. A feeling of inferiority creeps in.

You then follow up with secondary actions that feed their doubts. Here it is often

to the ball. Look at the line. And make your stroke. Comfortable. Easy. It's as simple as that. In other words, the advice must be vague, to make certain it is not helpful. But, in general, if properly managed, the mere giving of advice is sufficient to place the gamesman in a practically invincible position.

THE COMPLETE UPMANSHIP, STEPHEN POTTER, 1950

Silence.—The way of replying to a polemical attack the most unpleasant for both parties is to get annoyed and stay silent: for the attacker usually interprets the silence as a sign of contempt.

FRIEDRICH NIETZSCHE, 1844–1900

There are other
ways to fray
nerves. During
the Gulf War,
President Bush
kept pronouncing
the name of the
Iraqi leader as
"SAD-am,"
which loosely
means "shoeshine
boy." On Capitol
Hill, the ritual
mispronunciation
of a member's
name is a
time-tested
way to rattle
opponents or
haze newcomers.
Lyndon Johnson
was a master
of the practice.
When Johnson
was Senate
majority leader,
writes J. McIver
Weatherford, he
applied it with
junior members
who voted the
wrong way:
"While slapping
the young chap
on the back
and telling him
he understood,
Johnson would
break his name
into shreds as a
metaphorical
statement of what
would happen

best to work covertly, getting other people, the media, or simple rumor to do the job for you. The endgame is deceptively simple: having piled up enough self-doubt to trigger a reaction, you stand back and let the target self-destruct. You must avoid the temptation to gloat or get in a last blow; at this point, in fact, it is best to act friendly, even offering dubious assistance and advice. Your targets' reaction will be an overreaction. Either they will lash out, make an embarrassing mistake, or reveal themselves too much, or they will get overly defensive and try too hard to please others, working all too obviously to secure their position and validate their self-esteem. Defensive people unconsciously push people away.

At this point your opening action, especially if it is only subtly aggressive, will be forgotten. What will stand out will be your rivals' overreaction and humiliation. Your hands are clean, your reputation unsullied. Their loss of position is your gain; you are one up and they are one down. If you had attacked them directly, your advantage would be temporary or nonexistent; in fact, your political position would be precarious: your pathetic, suffering rivals would win sympathy as your victims, and attention would focus on you as responsible for their undoing. Instead they must fall on their swords. You may have given them a little help, but to whatever extent possible in their own eyes, and certainly in everyone else's, they must have only themselves to blame. That will make their defeat doubly galling and doubly effective.

To win without your victim's knowing how it happened or just what you have done is the height of unconventional warfare. Master the art and not only will you find it easier to fight on two fronts at the same time, but your path to the highest ranks will be that much smoother.

if the disloyalty persisted."

THE ART OF POLITICAL WARFARE, JOHN PITNEY, JR., 2000

Image:
The Mask. Every performer on the crowded stage is wearing a mask—a pleasant, appealing face to show the audience. Should an apparently innocent bump from a fellow performer make a mask fall, a far less pleasant look will be revealed, and one that few will forget even after the mask is restored.

Authority: We often give our rivals the means of our own destruction. —*Aesop (sixth century B.C.)*

29

TAKE SMALL BITES
THE FAIT ACCOMPLI
STRATEGY

If you seem too ambitious, you stir up resentment in other people; overt power grabs and sharp rises to the top are dangerous, creating envy, distrust, and suspicion. Often the best solution is to take small bites, swallow little territories, playing upon people's relatively short attention spans. Stay under the radar and they won't see your moves. And if they do, it may already be too late; the territory is yours, a fait accompli. You can always claim you acted out of self-defense. Before people realize it, you have accumulated an empire.

Chien/
Development
(Gradual
Progress)
*This hexagram
is made up of
Sun (wood,
penetration)
above, i.e.,
without, and
Ken (mountain,
stillness) below,
i.e., within. A tree
on a mountain
develops slowly
according to the
law of its being
and consequently
stands firmly
rooted. This
gives the idea of
a development
that proceeds
gradually, step
by step. The
attributes of
the trigrams
also point to
this: within is
tranquility, which
guards against
precipitate
actions, and
without is
penetration,
which makes
development and
progress possible.*

THE I CHING,
CHINA, CIRCA
EIGHTH CENTURY
B.C.

Most people are conservative by nature. Desperate to keep what they have, they dread the unforeseen consequences and situations that conflict inevitably brings. They hate confrontation and try to avoid it.

Suppose there is something you want or need for your security and power. Take it without discussion or warning and you give your enemies a choice, either to fight or to accept the loss and leave you alone. Is whatever you have taken, and your unilateral action in taking it, worth the bother, cost, and danger of waging war? Which costs more, the war or the loss? Take something of real value and they will have to choose carefully. Take something small and marginal, though, and it is almost impossible for your opponents to choose battle. There are likely to be many more reasons for leaving you alone than for fighting over something small. You have played to your enemy's conservative instincts, which are generally stronger than their acquisitive ones. And soon your ownership of this property becomes a fait accompli, part of the status quo, which is always best left alone.

Sooner or later, as part of this strategy, you will take another small bite. This time your rivals are warier; they are starting to see a pattern. But what you have taken is once again small, and once again they must ask themselves if fighting you is worth the headache. Only nibble at what you want and you never spark enough anger, fear, or mistrust to make people overcome their natural reluctance to fight. Let enough time pass between bites and you will also play to the shortness of people's attention spans.

The key to the fait accompli strategy is to act fast and without discussion. If you reveal your intentions before taking action, you will open yourself to a slew of criticisms, analyses, and questions.

In the social world as in nature, anything of size and stability grows slowly. The piecemeal strategy is the perfect antidote to our natural impatience: it focuses us on something small and immediate, a first bite, then how and where a second bite can get us closer to our ultimate objective. It forces us to think in terms of a process, a sequence of connected steps and actions, no matter how small.

In masking your manipulations you can never go too far. So when you take a bite, even a small one, make a show of acting out of self-defense. It also helps to appear as the underdog. Give the impression your objectives are limited by taking a substantial pause between bites—exploiting people's short attention spans—while proclaiming to one and all that you are a person of peace. In fact, it would be the height of wisdom to make your bite a little larger upon occasion and then giving back some of what you have taken. People see only your generosity and your limited actions, not the steadily increasing empire you are amassing.

Ambition can creep as well as soar.

EDMUND BURKE (1729–1797)

All the conceptions born of impatience and aimed at obtaining speedy victory could only be gross errors. . . . It was necessary to accumulate thousands of small victories to turn them into a great success.

GENERAL VO NGUYEN GIAP, 1911–

Image:
The Artichoke.
At first glance
it seems unappetizing,
even forbidding, with the
meager edible matter in its hard
exterior. The reward, however,
comes in taking it apart,
devouring it leaf by leaf. Its
leaves slowly become more
tender and tastier, until you
arrive at the succulent
heart.

Authority: To multiply small successes is precisely to build one treasure after another. In time one becomes rich without realizing how it has come about. —*Frederick the Great (1712–1786)*

30

PENETRATE THEIR MINDS
COMMUNICATION
STRATEGIES

Communication is a kind of war, its field of battle the resistant and defensive minds of the people you want to influence. The goal is to advance, to penetrate their defenses and occupy their minds. Anything else is ineffective communication, self-indulgent talk. Learn to infiltrate your ideas behind enemy lines, sending messages through little details, luring people into coming to the conclusions you desire and into thinking they've gotten there by themselves. Some you can trick by cloaking your extraordinary ideas in ordinary forms; others, more resistant and dull, must be awoken with extreme language that bristles with newness. At all cost, avoid language that is static, preachy, and overly personal. Make your words a spark for action, not passive contemplation.

KEYS TO WARFARE

For centuries people have searched for the magic formula that would give them the power to influence others through words. This search has been mostly elusive. Words have strange, paradoxical qualities: offer people advice, for instance, no matter how sound, and you imply that you know more than they do. To the extent that this strikes at their insecurities, your wise words may merely have the effect of entrenching them in the very habits you want to change. Once your language has gone out into the world, your audience will do what they want with it, interpreting it according to their own preconceptions.

Normal discourse, and even fine writing and art, usually only hits people on the surface. Our attempts to communicate with them become absorbed in all of the noise that fills their ears in daily life. The power to reach people more deeply, to alter their ideas and unpleasant behavior, is sometimes critical.

What you need to pay attention to is not simply the content of your communication but the form—the way you lead people to the conclusions you desire, rather than telling them the message in so many words. If you want to make people with low self-esteem feel better about themselves, praise has a superficial effect; instead you must prod them into accomplishing something tangible, giving them a real experience. That will translate into a much deeper feeling of confidence. Such indirect communication has the power to penetrate deep behind people's defenses.

In speaking this new language, learn to expand your vocabulary beyond explicit communication. Silence, for instance, can be used to great effect: by keeping quiet, not responding, you say a lot; by not mentioning something that people expect you to talk about, you call attention to this ellipsis, make it communicate. Similarly, the details in a text, speech, or work of art have great expressive power. In any period it can be dangerous to express ideas that go against the grain of public opinion or offend notions of correctness. It is best to seem to conform to these norms, then, by parroting the accepted wisdom, including the proper moral ending.

You can use details here and there to say something else. If you are writing a novel, for instance, you might put your dangerous opinions in the mouth of the villain but express them with such energy and color that they become more interesting than the speeches of the hero. Not everyone will understand your innuendos and layers of meaning, but some certainly will, at least those with the proper discernment; and mixed messages will excite your audience: indirect forms of expression— silence, innuendo, loaded details, deliberate blunders—make people feel as if they were participating, uncovering the meaning on their own. The more that people participate in the communication process, the more deeply they internalize its ideas.

In putting this strategy into practice, avoid the common mistake of straining to get people's attention by using a form that is shocking or strange. The attention you get this way will be superficial and short-lived. By using a form that alienates a wide public, you narrow your audience; you will end up preaching to the converted. Using a conventional form is more effective in the long run,

The Lydian King Croesus had had Miltiades much in his thoughts so when he learned of his capture, he sent a command to the people of Lampsacus to set him at liberty; if they refused, he was determined, he added, to "cut them down like a pine-tree." The people of the town were baffled by Croesus' threat, and at a loss to understand what being cut down like a pine-tree might mean, until at last the true significance of the phrase dawned upon a certain elderly man: the pine, he explained, was the only kind of tree which sent up no new shoots after being felled—cut down a pine and it will die off completely. The explanation made the Lampsacenes

so frightened of
Croesus that they
let Miltiades go.

THE HISTORIES,
HERODOTUS,
484–432 B.C.

because it attracts a larger audience. Once you have that audience, you can insinuate your real (and even shocking) content through details and subtext.

In war almost everything is judged by its result. If a general leads his army to defeat, his noble intentions do not matter; nor does the fact that unforeseen factors may have thrown him off course. He lost; no excuse will do. This standard can be applied to politics: what matters is not what people say or intend but the results of their actions, whether power is increased or decreased. Deeds and results do not lie. You must learn to apply the same barometer to your attempts at communication, and to those of other people.

The ability to reach people and alter their opinions is a serious affair, as serious and strategic as war. You must be harsher on yourself and on others: failure to communicate is the fault not of the dull-witted audience but of the unstrategic communicator.

Image: The Stiletto. It is long and tapered to a point. It requires no sharpening. In its form lies its perfection as an instrument to penetrate cleanly and deeply. Whether thrust into the flank, the back, or through the heart, it has a fatal effect.

Authority: I cannot give birth to wisdom myself and the accusation that many make against me, that while I question others, I myself bring nothing wise to light due to my lack of wisdom, is accurate. The reason for this is as follows: God forces me to serve as a midwife and prevents me from giving birth. *—Socrates (470–399 B.C.)*

31

DESTROY FROM WITHIN
THE INNER-FRONT STRATEGY

A war can only really be fought against an enemy who shows himself. By infiltrating your opponents' ranks, working from within to bring them down, you give them nothing to see or react against—the ultimate advantage. From within, you also learn their weaknesses and open up possibilities of sowing internal dissension. So hide your hostile intentions. To take something you want, do not fight those who have it, but rather join them—then either slowly make it your own or wait for the moment to stage a coup d'état. No structure can stand for long when it rots from within.

Throughout his revolutionary and missionary travels, Hasan [leader of the Nizari Ismailis] was searching for an impregnable fortress from which to conduct his resistance to the Seljuk empire. In about 1088, he finally chose the castle of Alamut, built on a narrow ridge on a high rock in the heart of the Elburz Mountains in a region known as the Rudbar. The castle dominated an enclosed cultivated valley thirty miles long and three miles across at its widest, approximately six thousand feet above sea level. Several villages dotted the valley, and their inhabitants were particularly receptive to the ascetic piety of Hasan. The castle was

The most common form of defense in old-fashioned warfare was the fortress or walled city, and military leaders strategized for centuries about how to take such structures. The conventional strategy against the fortress was to scale or breach its walls, using siege engines and battering rams. Often that meant first besieging it. The city's inhabitants would slowly starve and weaken, making it possible eventually to breach the walls and take the castle.

Over the centuries, however, certain enlightened strategists hit upon a different way to bring down the walls. Their strategy was based on a simple premise: the apparent strength of the fortress is an illusion, for behind its walls are people who are trapped, afraid, even desperate. The city's leaders have essentially run out of options; they can only put their faith in the fortress's architecture. To lay siege to these walls is to mistake the appearance of strength for reality. If in fact the walls are hiding great weakness within, then the proper strategy is to bypass them and aim for the interior. This can be done literally, by digging tunnels beneath the walls, undermining their strength—a conventional military strategy. A better, more devious route is to infiltrate people inside them or to work with the city's disaffected inhabitants. This is known as "opening an inner front"—finding a group on the inside who will work on your behalf to spread discontent and will eventually betray the fortress into your hands, sparing you a long siege.

The basic principle here is that it is easiest to topple a structure—a wall, a group, a defensive mind—from the inside out. When something begins to rot or fall apart from within, it collapses of its own weight—a far better way to bring it down than ramming yourself against its walls. Confederates on the inside will provide valuable intelligence on the enemy's vulnerabilities. They will silently and subtly sabotage him. They will spread internal dissension and division. The strategy can weaken the enemy to the point where you can finish him off with a penetrating blow; it can also bring down the enemy in and of itself.

A variation is to befriend your enemies, worming your way into their hearts and minds. As your targets' friend, you will naturally learn their needs and insecurities, the soft interior they try so hard to hide. Their guard will come down with a friend.

If there is someone on the inside whom you need to get rid of or thwart, the natural tendency is to consider conspiring with others in your group who feel the same way. In most conspiracies the goal is some large-scale action to topple the leader and seize power. The stakes are high, which is why conspiracies are so often difficult and dangerous. No matter how confident you may be of your fellow conspirators, you cannot know for certain what is going on in their minds.

There are a few precautions you can take. Keep the number of conspirators as small as possible. Involve them in the details of the plot only as necessary; the less they know, the less they have to blab. Revealing the schedule of your plan as late as possible before you all act will give them no time to back out.

accessible only with the greatest difficulty through a narrow gorge of the Alamut River. . . . Hasan employed a careful strategy to take over the castle, which had been granted to its current Shiite owner, named Mahdi, by the Seljuk sultan Malikshah. First, Hasan sent his trusted dai Husayn Qai-ni and two others to win converts in the neighboring villages. Next, many of the residents and soldiers of Alamut were secretly converted to Ismailism. Finally, in September 1090, Hasan himself was secretly smuggled into the castle. When Mahdi realized that Hasan had in fact quietly taken over his

fortress, he left
peacefully....

THE TEMPLARS
AND THE
ASSASSINS, JAMES
WASSERMAN, 2001

A prince
need trouble
little about
conspiracies
when the people
are well disposed,
but when they
are hostile and
hold him in
hatred, then
he must fear
everything and
everybody.

NICCOLÒ
MACHIAVELLI,
1469–1527

Finally, morale plays a crucial part in any war, and it is always wise to work to undermine the morale of the enemy troops. You can attempt this from the outside, through propaganda, but that often has the opposite effect, reinforcing the cohesion of soldiers and civilians in the face of an alien force trying to win them over. It is much more effective to find sympathizers within their ranks, who will spread discontent among them like a disease. Using an inner front to spread dissension is often enough to give you the advantage you need to overwhelm the enemy.

Image: The Termite. From deep within the structure of the house, the termite silently eats away at the wood, its armies patiently boring through beams and supports. The work goes unnoticed, but not the result.

Authority: The worst [military policy is] to assault walled cities. . . . If your commander, unable to control his temper, sends your troops swarming at the walls, your casualties will be one in three and still you will not have taken the city. . . . Therefore the expert in using the military subdues the enemy's forces without going to battle, takes the enemy's walled cities without launching an attack. *—Sun-tzu (fourth century B.C.)*

32

DOMINATE WHILE SEEMING TO SUBMIT THE PASSIVE-AGGRESSION STRATEGY

Any attempt to bend people to your will is a form of aggression. And in a world where political considerations are paramount, the most effective form of aggression is the best-hidden one: aggression behind a compliant, even loving exterior. To follow the passive-aggressive strategy, you must seem to go along with people, offering no resistance. But actually you dominate the situation. You are noncommittal, even a little helpless, but that only means that everything revolves around you. Some people may sense what you are up to and get angry. Don't worry— just make sure you have disguised your aggression enough that you can deny it exists. Do it right and they will feel guilty for accusing you. Passive aggression is a popular strategy; you must learn how to defend yourself against the vast legions of passive-aggressive warriors who will assail you in your daily life.

It is impossible to win a contest with a helpless opponent since if you win you have won nothing. Each blow you strike is unreturned so that all you can feel is guilt for having struck while at the same time experiencing the uneasy suspicion that the helplessness is calculated.

STRATEGIES OF PSYCHOTHERAPY, JAY HALEY, 1963

We humans have a particular limitation to our reasoning powers that causes us endless problems: when we are thinking about someone or about something that has happened to us, we generally opt for the simplest, most easily digestible interpretation. An acquaintance is good or bad, nice or mean, his or her intentions noble or nefarious; an event is positive or negative, beneficial or harmful; we are happy or sad. The truth is that nothing in life is ever so simple. People are invariably a mix of good and bad qualities, strengths and weaknesses. Their intentions in doing something can be helpful and harmful to us at the same time, a result of their ambivalent feelings toward us. Even the most positive event has a downside.

This tendency of ours to judge things in simple terms explains why passive aggression is so devilishly effective as a strategy and why so many people use it—consciously and unconsciously. By definition, people who are acting passive-aggressively are being passive and aggressive simultaneously. They are outwardly compliant, friendly, obedient, even loving. At the same time, they inwardly plot and take hostile action. Their aggression is often quite subtle—little acts of sabotage, remarks designed to get under your skin. It can also be blatantly harmful.

When we are the victims of this behavior, we find it hard to imagine that both things are happening at the same time. We can manage the idea that someone can be nice one day and nasty the next; that is just called being moody. But to be nasty and nice simultaneously—that confuses us. Our confusion gives the passive-aggressive war-rior great manipulative power over us.

There are two kinds of passive aggres-sion. The first is conscious strategy. The sec-ond is a semiconscious or even unconscious behavior that people use all the time in the petty and not-so-petty matters of daily life. You may be tempted to forgive this second passive-aggressive type, who seems unaware of the effects of his or her actions or helpless to stop, but people often understand what they are doing far better than you imagine, and you are more than likely being taken in by their friendly and helpless exterior. We are generally too lenient with this second variety.

The key to using passive aggression as a conscious, positive strategy is the front you present to your enemies. They must never be able to detect the sullen, defiant thoughts that are going on inside of you.

Passive aggression has deep roots in mil-itary strategy, in what can be called the "false surrender". In war your enemies can never read your thoughts. They must make your appearance their guide, reading the signs you give off to decipher what you are thinking and planning. Meanwhile the surrender of an army tends to be followed by a great flood of emotion and a lowering of everyone's guard. The victor will keep an eye on the beaten troops but, exhausted by the effort it took to win, will be hugely tempted to be less wary than before. A clever strategist, then, may falsely surrender—announce that he is defeated in body and spirit. Seeing no indica-tion otherwise, and unable to read his mind, the enemy is likely to take his submission

At times one has to deal with hidden enemies, intangible influences that slink into dark corners and from this hiding affect people by suggestion. In instances like this, it is necessary to trace these things back to the most secret recesses, in order to determine the nature of the influences to be dealt with. . . . The very anonymity of such plotting requires an especially vigorous and indefatigable effort, but this is well worth while. For when such elusive influences are brought into the light and branded, they lose their power over people.

THE I CHING, CHINA, CIRCA EIGHTH CENTURY B.C.

*In those days
force and arms
did prevail; but
now the wit
of the fox is
everywhere on
foot, so hardly
a faithful or
virtuous man
may be found.*

QUEEN
ELIZABETH I,
1533–1603

at face value. Now the false surrenderer has time and space to plot new hostilities.

In war as in life, the false surrender depends on the seamless appearance of submission. To make this work, you must do likewise: play up your weakness, your crushed spirit, your desire to be friends—an emotional ploy with great power to distract. You must also be something of an actor. Any sign of ambivalence will ruin the effect.

Remember: it is never wise to seem too eager for power, wealth, or fame. Your ambition may carry you to the top, but you will not be liked and will find your unpopularity a problem. Better to disguise your maneuvers for power: you do not want it but have found it forced upon you. Being passive and making others come to you is a brilliant form of aggression.

Subtle acts of sabotage can work wonders in the passive-aggressive strategy because you can camouflage them under your friendly, compliant front.

Passive aggression is so common in daily life that you have to know how to play defense as well as offense. By all means use the strategy yourself; it is too effective to drop from your armory. But you must also know how to deal with those semiconscious passive-aggressive types so prevalent in the modern world, recognizing what they are up to before they get under your skin and being able to defend yourself against this strange form of attack.

A colleague is warm to your face but says things behind your back that cause you problems. You let someone into your life who proceeds to steal something valuable of yours. These types do harm but are excellent at avoiding any kind of blame. Their modus operandi is to create enough doubt that they were the ones who did the aggressive act; it is never their fault. Somehow they are innocent bystanders, helpless, the real victims in the whole dynamic. Their denials of responsibility are confusing: you suspect they have done something, but you cannot prove it, or, worse, if they are *really* skillful, you feel guilty for even thinking them at fault. The guilt you feel is a sign of the power they have over you.

To defeat the passive-aggressive warrior, you must first work on yourself. This means being acutely aware of the blame-shifting tactic as it happens. Squash any feelings of guilt it might begin to make you feel. These types can be very ingratiating, using flattery to draw you into their web, preying on your insecurities. It is often your own weakness that sucks you into the passive-aggressive dynamic. Be alert to this.

Second, the smartest move is to disengage, at best to get the person out of your life, or at the least to not flare up and cause a scene, all of which plays into his hands. You need to stay calm.

The most effective counterstrategy with the passive-aggressive is often to be subtle and underhanded right back at them, neutralizing their powers. You must never leave the passive-aggressive time and space in which to operate. Let them take root and they will find all kinds of sly ways to pull you here and there. Your best defense is to be sensitive to any passive-aggressive manifestations in those around you and to keep your mind as free as possible from their insidious influence.

Image: The River. It flows with great force, sometimes flooding its banks and creating untold damage. Try to dam it and you only add to its pent-up energy and increase your risk. Instead divert its course, channel it, make its power serve your purposes.

Authority: As dripping water wears through rock, so the weak and yielding can subdue the firm and strong. —*Sun Haichen, Wiles of War (1991)*

33

SOW UNCERTAINTY AND PANIC THROUGH ACTS OF TERROR
THE CHAIN-REACTION STRATEGY

Terror is the ultimate way to paralyze a people's will to resist and destroy their ability to plan a strategic response. Such power is gained through sporadic acts of violence that create a constant feeling of threat, incubating a fear that spreads throughout the public sphere. The goal in a terror campaign is not battlefield victory but causing maximum chaos and provoking the other side into desperate overreaction. Melting invisibly into the population, tailoring their actions for the mass media, the strategists of terror create the illusion that they are everywhere and therefore that they are far more powerful than they really are. It is a war of nerves. The victims of terror must not succumb to fear or even anger; to plot the most effective counterstrategy, they must stay balanced. In the face of a terror campaign, one's rationality is the last line of defense.

"Brothers," says an Ismaili poet, "when the time of triumph comes, with good fortune from both worlds as our companion, then by one single warrior on foot a king may be stricken with terror, though he own more than a hundred thousand horsemen."

QUOTED IN *THE ASSASSINS*, BERNARD LEWIS, 1967

KEYS TO WARFARE

In the course of our daily lives, we are subject to fears of many kinds. These fears are generally related to something specific: someone might harm us, a particular problem is brewing, we are threatened by disease or even death itself. In the throes of any deep fear, our willpower is momentarily paralyzed as we contemplate the bad that could happen to us. If this condition lasted too long or were too intense, it would make life unbearable, so we find ways to avoid these thoughts and ease our fears. The distractions of daily life become the ground beneath us, keeping us upright and able to walk on without the paralysis that fear can bring.

Under certain circumstances, however, this ground can fall away from under us, and then there is nothing we can do to steady ourselves. What troubles us most is the uncertain future, the fear that more terrible things are coming and that we might soon suffer some unpredictable tragedy. Fear becomes chronic and intense, our minds besieged by all kinds of irrational thoughts. The specific fears become more general. Among a group, panic will set in.

In essence, this is terror: an intense, overpowering fear that we cannot manage or get rid of in the normal way. There is too much uncertainty, too many bad things that can happen to us.

It is a law of war and strategy that in the search for an advantage, anything will be tried and tested. And so it is that groups and individuals, seeing the immense power that terror can have over humans, have found a way to use terror as a strategy.

Although terror as a strategy can be employed by large armies and indeed whole states, it is most effectively practiced by those small in number. Being so few, they cannot hope to wage a conventional war or even a guerrilla campaign. Terror is their strategy of last resort. Taking on a much larger enemy, they are often desperate, and they have a cause to which they are utterly committed. Ethical considerations pale in comparison. And creating chaos is part of their strategy.

This asymmetry brings war to its ultimate extreme: the smallest number of people waging war against an enormous power, leveraging their smallness and desperation into a potent weapon. The dilemma that all terrorism presents, and the reason it attracts so many and is so potent, is that terrorists have a great deal less to lose than the armies arrayed against them, and a great deal to gain through terror.

In essence, terrorists kick a rock in order to start an avalanche. If no landslide follows, little is lost, except perhaps their own lives, which they are willing to sacrifice in their devotion to their cause. If mayhem and chaos ensue, though, they have great power to influence events. The ability to effect some kind of change, to attain a limited goal, is what makes terrorism so alluring, particularly to those who are otherwise powerless.

Terrorism is usually born out of feelings of weakness and despair, combined with a conviction that the cause one stands for, whether public or personal, is worth both the inflicting and the suffering of any kind of damage. A world in which the faces of power are often large and apparently invulnerable

When a man has learned within his heart what fear and trembling mean, he is safeguarded against any terror produced by outside influences. Let the thunder roll and spread terror a hundred miles around: he remains so composed and reverent in spirit that the sacrificial rite is not interrupted. This is the spirit that must animate leaders and rulers of men—a profound inner seriousness from which all outer terrors glance off harmlessly.

THE I CHING, CHINA, CIRCA EIGHTH CENTURY B.C.

We can no longer conceive of the idea of a symbolic calculation, as in poker or the potlatch: minimum stake, maximum result. This is exactly what the terrorists have accomplished with their attack on Manhattan, which illustrates rather well the theory of chaos: an initial shock, provoking incalculable consequences.

THE SPIRIT OF TERRORISM, JEAN BAUDRILLARD, 2002

only makes the strategy more appealing. In this sense terrorism can become a kind of style, a mode of behavior that filters down into society itself.

Yet for all its strengths, terrorism also has limitations that have proved the death of many a violent campaign, and those opposing it must know and exploit this. The strategy's main weakness is the terrorists' lack of ties to the public or to a real political base. Often isolated, living in hiding, they are prone to lose contact with reality, overestimating their own power and overplaying their hand. Although their use of violence must be strategic to succeed, their alienation from the public makes it hard for them to maintain a sense of balance. Accentuating the terrorists' isolation and denying them a political base should be part of any effective counterstrategy against them.

People who feel weak and powerless are often tempted into outbursts of anger or irrational behavior, which keeps those around them in suspense as to when the next attack will come. These fits of temper, like other, more serious kinds of terror, can have a chilling effect on their targets, sapping the will to resist; when the simplest dealings with these people are potentially so unpleasant, why fight? Why not just give in? A violent temper or outlandish act, volcanic and startling, can also create the illusion of power, disguising actual weaknesses and insecurities. And an emotional or out-of-control response to it just plays into the other person's hands, creating the kind of chaos and attention he or she thrives on. If you have to deal with a terroristic spouse or boss, it is best to fight back in a determined but dispassionate manner—the response such types least expect.

To combat terrorism it is always tempting to resort to a military solution, fighting violence with violence, showing the enemy that your will is not broken and that any future attacks on their part will come with a heavy price. The problem here is that terrorists by nature have much less to lose than you do. A counterstrike may hurt them but will not deter them; in fact, it may even embolden them and help them gain recruits. Terrorists are often willing to spend years bringing you down. To hit them with a dramatic counterstrike is only to show your impatience, your need for immediate results, your vulnerability to emotional responses—all signs not of strength but of weakness.

Because of the extreme asymmetry of forces at play in the terrorist strategy, the military solution is often the least effective. Terrorists are vaporous, spread out, linked not physically but by some radical and fanatic idea.

The French writer Raymond Aron defines terrorism as an act of violence whose psychological impact far exceeds its physical one. This psychological impact, however, then translates into something physical—panic, chaos, political division—all of which makes the terrorists seem more powerful than they are in reality. Any effective counterstrategy must take this into consideration.

Time must be taken to patiently uproot the terrorist threat. More valuable than military force here is solid intelligence, infiltration of the enemy ranks (working to find dissidents from within), and slowly and steadily drying up the money and resources on which the terrorist depends.

At the same time, it is important to occupy the moral high ground. As the victim of the attack, you have the advantage here, but you may lose it if you counterattack aggressively. Patient resolve and the refusal to overreact will serve as their own deterrents. Feelings of panic and hysteria reveal the degree to which the enemy has triumphed, as does an overly rigid attempt at defense, in which a society and culture at large are made hostage to a handful of men.

Image: The Tidal Wave. Something disturbs the water far out at sea—a tremor, a volcano, a landslide. A wave a few inches high begins to ripple, cresting into a larger wave and then a larger one still, the depth of the water giving it momentum, until it breaks on shore with an unimaginable destructive force.

Authority: There is no fate worse than being continuously under guard, for it means you are always afraid. —*Julius Caesar (100–44 B.C.)*

Also by Robert Greene

The Concise
48 Laws of Power

'Teaches you how to cheat, dissemble, feign, fight and advance your cause in the modern world' *Independent on Sunday*

978 1 86197 404 4

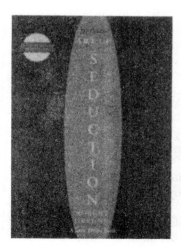

The Concise
Art of Seduction

'What Greene does so masterfully in his book is to take us on a fascinating trip into the psyches of the great seducers and offer a wealth of strategies for those who might like to dabble in the murky waters of manipulation themselves' *Daily Mail*

978 1 86197 641 3